I0562938

# MURDER IN YELLOWSTONE

## SARA FLORES, WEREWOLF P.I.

## SUE DENVER

JGF PRESS

# PRAISE FOR SUE DENVER'S WEREWOLF P.I. SERIES

"Sue Denver has the most unique and amazing plot lines."

— *FACEBOOK REVIEWER*

"Sue Denver has written a fascinating character in Sara. She reminds me of Jane Yellowrock from Faith Hunter's series, and in all the right ways: strong, aloof, in control of herself (until she isn't), and mysterious."

— MJ SILVERSMITH, *DISCOVERY*

"Riveting, thought-provoking mysteries that go one step beyond the usual whodunit (or, who will do it) scenarios.
*Midwest Book Review*

"Sara is one of my favorite heroines I've ever followed in any book ever!" *Amazon Reviewer*

"A bad-ass female getting the upper hand and beating powerful, rich, bad guys." *Amazon Reviewer*

# CONTENTS

# SARA FLORES' WORLD

- Sara's world is our everyday, normal world.
- Nobody believes in werewolves, vampires or anything supernatural.
- Sara was turned into a werewolf by her former neighbor Joe White Wolf — right before he died.
- Sara thinks she's the only werewolf on earth, but she hopes (or fears) she's wrong.
- Lupiti elders remember their grandfathers talk about seeing old Joe White Wolf turn into a wolf during tribal ceremonies — way back in the late 1800's.
- This tells Sara she may have a very, very long life — if her new lifestyle doesn't get her killed.

# PROLOGUE

## 11 YEARS AGO

**O**tto Hawking awoke to a blinding headache and complete blackness. His body was bouncing up and down and his head hit on a spot so sore it couldn't have been the first time.

Where was he?

There was the harsh whine of a chainsaw... no... a snowmobile.

He tried to sit up, but his arms and legs were slow to respond and could move only inches. He was trapped in something soft... a blanket? And... were straps holding him down?

He blinked his eyes and shook his head. His brain was foggy. He was tied up like cargo and someone was moving him on a snowmobile.

Where?

More importantly — why?

He took stock. *I'm Otto Hawking. I'm in... Big Sky, Montana? No... I'd left there. I was going... I was driving...*

His head spun and he gasped for breath.

He laughed, then stopped suddenly.

*That was weird. This was not funny.*

Where was he... Yes! He'd stopped for the night in West Yellowstone, Montana. He was going home to Oklahoma.

But why?

He liked his life in Big Sky. He had good work and he'd found a good woman. Why would he be going back to Oklahoma and the wife who married him instead of the man she really loved?

Hell no, he wouldn't go back to her. Going back made no sense.

He shivered. He was cold, even wrapped in a blanket. Maybe he should just sleep awhile. The idea sounded wonderful.

"Ow!" He awoke again as his head bounced on that same painful spot.

He tried to roll over but his body was strangely limp and slow to obey him. He struggled.

His hands and feet were tied together! Not with flex ties — nothing was cutting into his body. Something wider. Something that wouldn't leave marks?

*Think! What is going on?*

He gasped again for breath — as if he'd been running for miles.

Was someone taking him to a doctor? It was a funny way to go to the doctor.

He started to laugh.

No! He forced his mouth to stop smiling. His wrists and ankles were bound. How could he have forgotten that? What was wrong with him?

He was in deep trouble.

"No shit, Sherlock," he said, laughing again.

Suddenly, the snowmobile started climbing and he was slammed back against something metal. His nose hit hard and he saw stars.

Gosh, they were pretty. Red stars mixed in with the white ones.

He bounced more as the terrain got rougher. The chainsaw whine was even louder.

Then it shut off.

They were still.

The world was silent. Not a sound anywhere.

Otto bounced as the driver got off the machine. His head jerked when someone grabbed the cloth around it, and suddenly he could see. The white lights of the snowmobile nearly blinded him, so he turned away. He was fastened to the floor up against three seats that sat behind the driver's seat.

It was night and snowflakes fell on his face — leaving wet spots so cold they burned.

He smiled. *My god it was gorgeous.*

Suddenly a man's face popped into his view, hanging over him.

"You!" Otto said, a wave of tension flooding him. "You!"

The man released one of the clasps and jerked Otto to a sitting position. Then he released the bindings over his legs.

Otto struggled, but the blanket — it *was* a blanket — still held him. The man grabbed him and jerked him off the snowmobile — letting him drop onto the snow-covered ground.

Otto struggled and kicked, his heart racing, his lungs gulping for more air. His heart pounded with fear. And he was angry.

Finally — finally! — he escaped the blanket.

"What's wrong with you?" he asked, managing to sit up.

A wave of nausea hit him and he spewed vomit onto the man. He rolled away and vomited again.

He looked up and saw the look on the man's face — which made him laugh.

The man grimaced in hatred and he stepped toward Otto. He raised his boot, aiming his kick, but... he jerked to a stop.

"Goddamnit!" the man said, his entire body shaking with the need to kick Otto. "It's bad enough I have to waste four cold hours out here to dump you, but now this?"

Otto looked up at him. He was afraid he knew the answer, but he asked anyway, "Why didn't you kick me?"

"Can't leave any marks," the man said.

Just as Otto feared. "I wasn't going to do anything about what I heard. This is unnecessary."

"I got my orders." The man grabbed the blanket from the ground and stowed it back on the snowmobile. Then he reached inside his jacket and removed a syringe.

*I've been drugged*, Otto realized. *Of course — no wonder I can't think straight.*

And now the man would finish the job. Unless... Otto had just one chance — maybe.

He sat back in the snow and held his stomach, groaning. Trying to look more helpless.

The man came towards him, and Otto raised his tied hands and grabbed the man's arm. He'd always had a very strong grip, but tonight... tonight his arms felt like noodles. He tried to hold on but the man easily pushed him off, shoved him back in the snow, and jabbed the needle into his neck.

He pulled out a knife and cut away the bindings on Otto's hands and legs, putting the cloth remnants into one of his pockets. Then he patted Otto down and removed his cell phone, which he laid on a snow-covered rock and smashed with his boot.

He climbed back on the snowmobile.

Otto took stock. He had a leather jacket, no gloves, nothing for his head, and cowboy boots. They had some tread on them — he wouldn't slip and slide on the ice. But they wouldn't keep out the water for very long.

"Hawking," the man said.

Otto looked up.

"You're eight miles inside Yellowstone, past an entrance that is closed for the winter. There's nobody anywhere around and nobody coming. You can waste your last minutes trying to walk out if you want. Up to you."

The man turned the sled and headed away, darkness returning as his lights dimmed and then disappeared.

The whine of the snowmobile lasted a little longer, then faded away leaving a smothering silence.

Otto imagined he could feel the drug moving through his body, dimming the lights in his brain, turning down the energy in each muscle, one by one, draining him.

He considered building a snow cave, but his body was wet. He'd sweated in fear, and his wet body would kill him quickly — snow cave or not.

He rose to his feet. He'd walked eight miles before. He'd walked fifty. He could do it again. But his knees trembled, and his legs collapsed beneath him.

He had no paper or pen he could write with. No way to tell anyone what had happened to him. He'd always dictated ideas to his phone. He crawled to the rock where the pieces of it lay. He could see the phone had sent its last message.

*So*, he thought. *This was it.*

What the hell does a man do when facing his death? If he was Pawnee or Apache or most of the Plains tribes — he'd sing a death song. But Otto was Lupiti. They didn't have death songs — at least not as far as he knew.

Then, soft, far away, Otto heard a howl. One of the Yellowstone wolves. A second wolf joined in. Then another.

Now there was a chorus of howls.

How did they do that?

Each wolf's song was separate — a wolf's own choice of pitch, length, and movement up and down the scale. And yet they meshed into a single melody. Almost a group prayer. Or celebration. Or... a belonging ceremony.

The wolf was Otto's spirit animal. He chose it — or it chose him — when he was just a boy. But he hadn't thought about it in a long time. After all, what practical value did a spirit animal have in today's world?

And, yet...

There they were. Almost like they were sending him off to the next world. Otto smiled.

Then he laughed.

It had to be the drug.

Otto wondered what he'd been given. He'd been stupidly happy since he woke up tonight. Well... if you had to die... stupidly happy was better than most of the alternatives.

Otto shook his head. He couldn't die. If he did — the man he'd overheard would get away with murder.

He'd lied to the man. He'd left a letter with an attorney to send if he died. He was glad of that now.

But would it get Lydia in trouble? He needed to protect her.

How?

He couldn't have more than minutes left to live.

Already he could feel the tiredness creeping up on him. His body was urging him to give up and drift off to a wonderful sleep.

"Dakota," he cried. "Dakota, my cherished daughter."

He'd left her with his wife. Emily was a good woman and a good mother. She might have been a good wife — to the man she really loved. All his life, he'd never felt he could please her. He'd believed he wasn't good enough. Only to find out he *never* could have pleased her.

He hadn't been able to look at her after that.

But he'd planned to come back for Dakota once she was 18. To let her know she was always in his heart.

She was only seven now.

Otto noticed the wolf chorus had stopped. He was so sleepy. Surprisingly, he was no longer cold.

He sat up on his knees so he could stay awake as long as possible. He spread his hands out and looked up into the stars.

Otto prayed to the Great Spirit.

He didn't know how — he'd never done it before.

He asked his spirit animal — the wolves — to intercede for him. To look out for his little girl. To let her know of his love.

Otto prayed until the drugs pulled him into sleep, and he fell over.

Ten minutes later, the spirits took him away.

# 1

## SARA FLORES, CURRENT DAY

I was sitting in my one-room, private investigator office in downtown Tulsa, Oklahoma, with my cowboy boots up on my crappy desk, reminiscing about our successful last case. We'd stopped a sex trafficking ring, found our client's daughter, and rescued several other young women.

Who am I? My name is Sara Flores and I'm a reasonably attractive 5' 7", 30-something with shaggy dark hair. I'm a private investigator, a calling I've found after being turned into a werewolf.

Since everyone knows there's no such thing as werewolves, I guard that secret like it means my life — because it probably does.

I was in a good mood because our office war chest was topped off with a new $14 million that my tech guru/partner Mason Spencer had stolen from a scumbag billionaire who had purchased four of the women. The man didn't need that hidden bank account anymore — being as how his body was currently feeding fishes at the bottom of the Gulf of Mexico.

My watch told me it was 5:30 P.M., about time to go home to my wolf-dog Skidi. I was looking forward to a nice, long walk with her — especially because Tulsa temperatures today hit a high of 55 degrees. Not bad for January 11.

In sum, I felt on top of the world.

Until Bill Hanalho walked into my office.

I stood up, surprised to see him.

Bill is the current priest of the Lupiti Nation, a position held before him by his grandfather and his grandfather's grandfather. To continue that lineage, Bill needs to marry a Lupiti woman.

Why is that important? Because I am not Lupiti. Which is the only reason I haven't already tumbled into bed with him and — I'd like to think — the only reason he hasn't returned the favor.

It was also the reason we typically talk on the phone instead of meeting in person. That way I wouldn't be face-to-face with his long, black hair hanging halfway to his waist. Or his body — six feet of Western male in well-worn blue jeans and boots.

Tonight he was wearing a light-blue flannel shirt that looked softer than a cloud. It covered what I knew to be the finest-looking male chest I'd ever seen.

My mouth was dry, and I tried to swallow.

"Sara," he said.

"Bill."

Silence hung between us.

"Sara," Bill said. "I... there's a girl who's gone missing. She was seeking answers about her father. It's... complicated. I think you're the only one with a chance of helping her."

It took me a second to decipher his words. "A client, you mean... sure."

I sat back down behind my desk. I couldn't be disappointed. After all, this was what I did.

"Have a seat and tell me why you think only I can help her."

He sat down and crossed an ankle over one knee. I jerked my eyes back up to his.

I hated how he made me stupid.

"Her name is Dakota Hawking," Bill said. "She came to me because she was seeing visions about her father alone in a snowstorm. She felt someone was trying to kill him."

He hesitated.

I waited.

"Dakota believes her father was trying to communicate with her...." He trailed off.

"And?"

"He's dead. He died 11 years ago in a snowstorm in Montana — just inside Yellowstone Park."

I nodded, "I understand why you came to me."

Two years ago, I had my one run-in with this woo-woo talk-to-the-dead stuff. I'd been reading historical papers about Lupiti Ceremonies — trying to find out more about Joe White Wolf, the man who turned me and then died on me without telling me a damn thing about my new condition. Joe was a shaman and there were ceremonies recorded where a Lupiti shaman could supposedly turn into a wolf.

But I'd also read about different ceremonies held by Lupiti priests, some of whom were supposed to be able to talk to the dead.

I'd swallowed too much champagne alone the New Year's Eve night before and got the "brilliant" idea to contact Joe from the dead to ask him, basically, WTF!

Bill's grandfather performed the ceremony, and I actually did hear Joe in my mind — although he wasn't interested in my questions. He wanted me to kill Bill's grandfather, who, it turns out, had been his arch-enemy.

My brain was mushed with peyote and whatever else they had me drink for the ceremony, but the upshot was that I got no answers to my questions. And the priest died.

And no, I didn't kill him.

"Obviously, I know it's possible," I said. "But I don't... I wouldn't have a clue how to help you."

"Think of her as a normal missing-person case. A girl who went to investigate her father's death and has now disappeared. You just needed to know the father's message because, although his death was ruled an accident, it's possible he was murdered."

I nodded. "Which would make it more likely her disappearance is connected to his death."

"I'm afraid for Dakota's life."

"I'll talk to her mother tomorrow morning," I said.

Bill sat there.

I looked at him. "What else?"

"You'll meet her. Draw your own conclusions." He stood up. "Thank you."

Bill stared at me, then turned and left.

I realized we never touch when we meet or say goodbye. No handshake. No kiss on the cheek. No pat on the back.

I don't know his reasons, but I was afraid touching him might burn me.

# 2

---

## SARA

I was beyond curious to meet Dakota's mother, Emily Hawking, and not just because of Bill's cryptic comment.

I called her last night to set up an appointment, and she had refused me. She said the police had been notified her daughter was missing and she had no interest in talking to a private investigator.

She only agreed to meet when I said Bill Hanalho had asked me to talk to her.

It was another example of how important he was to the Lupiti Nation. He seems like a normal guy when you meet him, but he carries real weight in his community.

The day was clear, heading into the 50s again as I drove into the town of Lupiti. My former home in Colorado was being hit by a blizzard today, so I gave myself a pat on the back for leaving that weather behind.

Oh, Tulsa had snow. Occasionally. Sometimes even half an inch — which typically shut down the city.

I passed one tract house after another on Emily Hawking's street, right up until it dead-ended at her place, which sat on twice the land her neighbors had. The house was small, but money had added style. There was a low stone wall, pillars and a generous front porch. The roof had a two-window dormer set into it, making it the only house on the street with a second floor.

The lawn in front was mowed, but tall bushes surrounded the back of the house and crept around the sides as if they wanted to swallow it.

Emily Hawking was a striking woman in her early 40s, with long black hair and no makeup. She wore large, oval, beaded earrings and casual clothes, but her blouse was crisply pressed, and her jeans had an ironed crease in them. The earring design was duplicated on her expensive-looking moccasins.

Her mouth pursed, as if seeing me was distasteful.

I showed her my P.I. badge and, because she hadn't offered, I asked if I could come in.

This was very rude behavior for a Lupiti, and I bet myself she wouldn't offer me anything to drink — the rudest hospitality insult of all.

I won the bet — she offered nothing.

Her living room was sparse, the few furnishings in good taste and polished to gleam. By the window was a soft, high-backed chair with a book open on the coffee table and what looked like a cup of tea she'd just abandoned.

Unless she worked nights, she was unemployed — unusual for a widowed mother whose child had just turned 18.

The cup of tea meant she'd kick me out as soon as she could.

"What do you do for a living?" I asked her, returning her rudeness. A sudden hint of fear-sweat wafted from her.

Enhanced smell was one of my favorite gifts from my wolf.

I've confronted liars so good you would have bet the house on their truthfulness, but even the most accomplished of them knows they are lying. Humans have apocrine glands under their arms, and they reliably produce fear-stink. It's not noticeable to a human nose, but it's unmistakable to mine.

I read recently that the Department of Homeland Security in 2009 tried and failed to find a way to measure this as a lie detector.

Fortunately, they don't know about me.

She frowned at me and said, "I have a small insurance check from my husband's death. Not that it's any business of yours."

She motioned me to sit down on a sofa, then sat across from me, on the edge of her seat, as if she would spring up at any second.

"Fair enough," I said. "Why don't you want a private investigator looking for your daughter?"

Emily sighed theatrically. "This isn't the first time she's 'disappeared.' We've had our conflicts, like any mother and daughter, I suppose. Dakota has told me repeatedly in the last six months that she's 18 now. An adult. But... just in case it's real this time, I filed a police report and they have talked to the police in Montana."

I nodded. "I understand all of that. But why wouldn't you want an investigator looking as well? Certainly, we can give it more attention than you are probably getting from the cops."

She waved a hand in dismissal. "I see no reason to pay for it."

"As a favor to Bill Hanahlo, my office is prepared to charge you only a single dollar." (This is how we use our office "war chest" — helping people who could not afford us.)

Emily frowned and rose.

I got up, too. "I have a form for you to sign. I need the one dollar so you're officially a client. That's the total you would ever owe."

She turned her back on me and walked to the door, opening it. She stood there, holding it, and glared at me.

I stood where I was and said, "Bill thinks Dakota's life is in danger."

She threw her hands up, exasperated. "Oh, that. Dakota's been filling his ears with her wishful thinking. She's told him Otto's been trying to contact her from the dead. I mean, *really*."

She looked at me. I stared back.

"Oh, you *can't* believe all that nonsense! Otto was careless somehow, and it cost him his life. The Wyoming police were very thorough, but Dakota won't believe that. She doesn't like that he died from some stupid mistake. It's much more dramatic if someone killed him. And even more dramatic if he's calling to her from beyond the grave."

I kept my position, so she waved at the door and said, "Come on now. I've heard enough."

I walked to her. "My understanding is Dakota went to Montana to investigate what happened to Otto, and now she's missing. Whether or not you believe in Otto communicating with your daughter, the police said his death was *probably* an accident. If someone killed him, her digging around means you could lose her too."

Her face was so close to mine that I could see tears form before her eyes darted away from me.

Her lips tightened. "Oh, alright." She left the door open and walked out of the room, coming back with a purse. She took out a $1 bill and held it out to me. "What else do you need?"

I pulled out the contract and showed her where to sign.

She inked her signature, then folded it back up and shoved it at me. She looked at the open door.

While I had a bunch of questions for her, I took the hint. I walked out of the house, closing the door. Without that contract, I would have no standing in the case.

I left before she could demand I return it.

I would have taken the case, regardless, because Bill asked. But after this meeting, I wanted the answers for myself. There's a reason I became a private investigator — I'm drawn to uncover or expose secrets.

Especially deadly ones.

# 3

## SARA

I'd rather have a root canal than walk into a police station. Any police station.

They were all filled with suspicious cops whose eyes were well-trained at detecting threats. If they knew what I was or even a fraction of the things I've done — I'd never get back out of the building.

Since I became a private eye, I found yet another thing to detest about the places. Cops look at P.I.'s like we are dog poop that got stuck on the bottom of their shoes.

I try — but usually fail — not to take it personally.

The Lupiti police station looked like a concrete-block jail, although at least someone painted it white. The windows were multipane grids not of wood but of reinforced steel.

Sergeant Alex Walker was more tolerable than the average cop. For one thing, he was easier on the eyes — a handsome man, pushing 40, with some Native blood showing in his cheekbones and shiny black hair.

I thought he might have a killer smile, but I had never seen it.

He also had a better attitude than most. Or at least he hid his opinions about P.I.s better. He even helped me with a case once — although grudgingly. He'd given me a good lead.

Today, he walked me back to the detective division — a small, depressing, puke-green room with three desks for the two detectives who served both the town and the Lupiti Nation.

I sat across from him, and he pushed two files to me.

I frowned and paged through them. One was for Otto Hawking and the other for Dakota. Inside of each were several pages, including copies of interviews and phone conversations.

I frowned harder and stared at him. He'd never been this helpful.

His mouth twisted and he said, "Yeah, well... Bill Hanalho stopped by here. He said you'd be coming to see me, and he asked me to help you."

"And you really *are* helping me?"

His mouth shifted to the side, hiding what looked like the start of a smile.

He narrowed his eyes. "Don't make me regret this."

My ears tingled. There was something in his voice when he said "regret."

I guessed, "You don't think her father's death was an accident, do you?"

He stared at me for long enough that I wasn't sure he would answer. Then he said, "The Otto I knew would never have gotten lost in a snowstorm. He respected nature. Lived in harmony with it. He was not an idiot."

"Tell me about his body. Obviously he had no bullets in him."

Again Walker half smiled. "Obviously. But since animals got to him, we can't know if he was stabbed."

He nodded his chin at the file I was holding. "Look at the toxicology report."

I did. My breath caught when I saw the part he wanted me to see. "He had Fentanyl in his system? How high a dose is this?"

"Moderate."

"So, not the cause of death?"

Walker shook his head at me. "We can't say. A fatal dose of fentanyl can kill some people more quickly than others. If it took longer, the post-mortem concentration in the body would be less."

"Do you know if he used recreationally?"

"You're never 100 percent sure, but I'd bet money he didn't. I never heard of him using and I typically would in this small of a community."

I flipped back in the files to the map I'd seen. "Where was he found?"

Walker took the map and pointed to a red dot. "Here. It's about eight miles inside Yellowstone Park from the West entrance — which was closed for the winter when he went missing. He was found in May when the snow melted."

I frowned. "How far from the nearest town or home?"

"Ten miles from the town of West Yellowstone."

"How did he get there? Car? Snowmobile? Horse?"

"None were found. His car wasn't seen after he checked into the hotel in town. The Sheriff's office there thinks he took a snowmobile on the closed and unplowed road into the Park and ran out of gas. His body was well off the road, so they think he set off walking to find shelter or fuel."

"And the snowmobile?"

"They think someone stole it — sometime before he was found."

"Had he rented it?"

"Not through any rental company."

"And how do they explain his missing car?"

"Also must have been stolen."

"I'm hearing a lot of coincidences. Someone steals his car in town and some other person steals whatever he took into the Park?"

Walker looked at his watch and stood up. I joined him, grabbing both files.

He started towards the door, saying, "All we have on Dakota so far are her credit charges since she left here in early September. You can track her from that."

"Why isn't the FBI involved?"

"She's not a minor, and kids her age go missing — on purpose — all the time. It's only been a week."

"'Only a week?' Do you know how much can go wrong in one week?"

Walker stopped and glared at me. "Of course I do. It's the only reason I'm talking to you."

"Sorry," I said. "And understood."

We walked to the exit, and I opened it.

Behind me, I heard, "Sara Flores."

I turned.

"Dakota's one of the good ones. Find her."

I nodded and let myself out, picking my secure phone out of my bag. I speed-dialed my computer guru and partner Mason Spencer. It was about five P.M. my time, an hour later at Mason's Pennsylvania home office. Since Mason's a night owl, it was the middle of his workday.

I got into my truck and spread out the files Walker gave me so Mason and I could discuss what we needed.

Mason could hack almost any system.

It was how we met. He'd hacked a company in Oklahoma with a big — murderous — secret to hide. Goons came for him, and Mason's Lupiti mother hired me to save her boy. I'd had to transform to do it, so Mason was one of three people who knew my secret.

Which was three more people than I was comfortable with.

After I explained, Mason said, "This is really two cases, isn't it? We probably have to solve what happened to Otto in order to find Dakota. But we have no time because if someone killed Otto and now has Dakota — she is either dead or likely to become dead soon."

"Exactly. We also have multiple Montana locations where Otto and then Dakota visited."

We both thought about that.

He said, "You'll need to pull in Connor and Judy for this case."

"Agreed." We'd used both of them on our last case and they were each valuable. "I'll call Judy tonight. You want to check on Connor? He said he was taking a bodyguard job until we got our next case."

"Also," I asked, "Can you get me a preliminary info dump on this case for tomorrow A.M.?"

"I'll drop it off in person. I'm taking a flight tonight."

"What?"

Mason had hung up.

This was beyond strange. The kid was based in Pennsylvania because the isolation suited him. Mason could get along socially... if he had to. For a short time. But people stressed him out, made him uncomfortable. Getting him to come to Tulsa was always a pain in the butt.

Now he was coming — voluntarily?

# 4

## MASON

Mason Spencer sat at the kitchen counter of his mom's Lupiti home, drank his yaupon tea for the caffeine, and tried to stop his fingers from drumming on the white laminate counter.

He opened his mouth to give her his usual complaint about the bright-yellow cabinets she thought looked like sunshine, and he thought looked like... well, never mind. But Aunt Emma's two boys crashed into him as they ran for the fridge, barely apologizing as they grabbed drinks and ran back outside to a soccer game that was careening madly all over the backyard.

He wished — fervently — he was back in Pennsylvania.

"I'm worried about you," his mom said.

Mason frowned at her. She'd summoned him across the country just for this?

And yet... as he looked at her, something was wrong.

Carole Red Eagle had been the mom his school friends envied. A motorcycle-riding illustrator of children's books with long black hair to her waist. She was young and beautiful, her eyes sparkling with love and interest and mischief.

Today... well... her eyes weren't sparkling. They looked tired. Even a little puffy. Okay, she was older now. Past 40. But she didn't look this old a week ago when they had dinner in Pennsylvania with his dad.

He shook himself. "I'm doing great. How many other 23-year-olds do you know who are partners in a business and making boatloads of money?"

She gave him that "mom smile" and patted his shoulder. "Yes, you make all the other moms jealous of your success."

Then she stared at him. "But, Mason, what about your life? What about love and family? And someday, kids?"

*Oh crap,* he thought, rubbing his eyes. "It's the wrong time to talk kids to me. Some brat kept kicking the seat behind me on the plane here — I didn't get more than 10 minutes of sleep."

"Are you seeing anyone?"

"Mom! I date."

"Pennsylvania girls. Who obviously aren't doing anything for you. Maybe you need to try Lupiti girls?"

"I'm just very busy these days. I don't have much time."

She sighed and sat down beside him, sipping her pink sumac lemonade.

"I know it's been hard for you," she said. "You're Lupiti like me, but you're also German like your father. I've watched you try to force yourself to fit into each of our worlds. I can see the struggle."

She turned to him. "I want you to do me a favor. Have I asked you for favors before?"

Mason's heart fell all the way down to his orange running sneakers. Grudgingly, he said, "None I can remember."

"I have the names and phone numbers of three nice Lupiti girls here." She put a paper in front of him. "I want you to go out with each of them while you're here. Give each one a chance."

She reached out and took his face in her hands and looked into his eyes. "Will you do that?"

He sighed. "Okay, Mom." He tried to turn away, but she held onto him.

"Mom?"

"Mason?"

He looked down. "Well, I can't do it this trip. Not enough time. But I will do it."

"This trip, my bravo. Promise me you'll do it this trip. I want to know you're on your way to a full, rich, happy life."

"Mom? Are you okay? Is anything wrong?"

"Of course, I'm okay. This is the one favor I want from you for all I did in raising you. I won't ask for another. Please, Mason."

"Alright. Alright. Mason leaned forward and kissed her on the cheek. Somehow I'll do it. Now I have to get to work."

He grabbed the list and got out of there as fast as he could without running.

In his rental car he rubbed his head with his hands and took a deep breath.

# 5

## SARA

I was sitting in my office with maps of Montana and Yellowstone Park spread out on my desk.

There was a knock at the door — which I keep locked — then a soft "click" my better-than-human ears heard as the door lock retracted.

My right hand opened the desk drawer where I had a new gun I was trying out. It was a 9 mm Glock that Full Conceal had modified so it folded in half to take up the size of a fat smartphone.

I snapped the grip into place, then held it out of sight.

The door opened and Mason Spencer stepped in. He got one look at me and theatrically raised his hands in the "don't shoot" position. "It's just me."

I put away the gun and looked at him.

"So," he said, sitting down across from me. "Let me tell you what I've found thus far…"

I held up my hand to stop him and asked, "What's wrong?"

"Nothing."

"Mason…"

He looked around. "I love what you've done to this place."

I scowled and he grinned. He knew how to push my buttons.

Our new employee Judy Street had bitched from day one about

how crappy and unprofessional my office looked. Now my clothes rack of disguises was gone, with big, impressive-looking cabinets in their place. She'd replaced my coffee table and chairs with some color-coordinated, way-too-fancy crap. The only original thing left was my desk, and I'd had to threaten her life to keep that.

"Yeah, yeah, yuck it up," I grumbled. "Maybe we should let her loose on your Command Central office in Pennsylvania."

"Horrors!" Mason said with a real shiver. "Don't you want to hear what I found on Emily Hawking? Where her money is coming from?"

Of course I did. "No 'small insurance payout' for Emily?"

"Otto didn't have an insurance policy," Mason said. "At least nothing I can find that he paid for. And yet, after Otto died, checks started hitting Emily's bank account for $3,000 a month. The amount has increased each year in tune with the cost of living index. Today she's getting $4,000 a month. That's about $1200 better than a livable wage here."

"The source?" I asked.

"AFJ Insurance. Ever heard of them?"

"No."

"Neither has anyone else. It's basically one attorney, based in Houston, who deposits the funds in Emily's account. He also handles payments for three other companies. All four businesses are wholly owned by a company based in Panama with no listing for corporate owners."

I raised my eyebrows at him. "Surely, the great Mason..."

He smirked and shrugged his shoulders. "I'm trying, obviously. But I might not be able to find who owns them. Panamanian law doesn't require the company to name any of its owners, so there's no paper trail to follow."

Mason sat hunched over my maps, avoiding my eyes.

"So, why are you in Tulsa?" I asked.

"I'm tracking Otto's car, but there's been no sign of it or his license plate in 11 years. You think he drove it into Yellowstone Park?"

I sighed. "He wouldn't have. The West entrance closes in early November and the road was piled deep with snow. The North entrance was open, but he would have had to drive 150 miles in a blizzard just to get there, then he'd have to drive another 50 to get to where his body was found."

Mason said, "West Yellowstone rents all sorts of ways he could have traveled. Snowmobiles, horses, cross-country skis and snow shoes."

"Or," I said, "someone could have used their private snowmobile to take him into the Park and kill him. Or dump the body if he was already dead."

Mason nodded. "Or he could have stolen somebody's snowmobile to escape — and froze to death. That person could have gone in later to find the vehicle and remove it. To make sure he wasn't connected to them."

"We have to find out who he met that he might have crossed."

I got up and opened my mini-fridge. I grabbed a diet cola for me and one of Mason's revolting lemon-lime sodas which, for some unknown reason, I always keep a couple of in my fridge. Even though he's rarely here.

I handed it to him, then instead of sitting behind my desk I sat down in a chair beside him.

I consider myself pretty clueless when it comes to men, despite (or maybe because of) one failed marriage. But one thing I have learned is that men with personal problems are more likely to discuss them if they don't have to look at you while they do it.

So, looking carefully off into the distance, I said, "C'mon, Mason. What's wrong?"

He took a big drink and then put his can on my desk. "My mom asked me to come here." He pulled a list out from his pocket and shoved it at me. I unfolded it and found three female names with short bios and phone numbers.

I shook my head at him, not understanding.

"She's trying to marry me off. She got my promise to take out each of these 'nice Lupiti girls.'"

"Oh hell," I blurted. "You're only 23."

He turned to me. "Exactly! Besides, I don't need help finding women. If I wanted to."

And just like that I found myself in sympathy with his mother.

Could Mason really find his own women? He was the most socially awkward male I'd ever met. Crazy, because girls would love his looks. His half-Lupiti heritage gave him long, wavy brown hair, dark brooding eyes, and a tall, lean body.

I thought of him as the kid brother I'd never had, but I realized he'd never once talked to me about a girl he was dating.

"Don't mothers do this kind of thing all the time?" I was on shaky ground here, since my mother died when I was 18.

"Not her. Not before today. She said I had to promise to see all three on this trip. That it was the only favor she would ask of me."

"So," he said. "You've got a credit card trail for Dakota. I can backtrack on that and see what video we can find. She was at the Ratikuk Reservation in Montana? What days?"

*Huh? So much for talking about his mother.*

I grabbed Dakota's file and looked. "Earliest charge there was September 15. Latest was September 20."

"They have a big event in the middle of September — Ratikuk Native Days. I'll bet I can find thousands of photos posted on the Internet from there. I'll run them through facial recognition and see if there was anyone with her. Or watching her."

Mason was talking just a little too fast. Like he did when he wanted you to ignore something. I knew I should mind my own business, but... I became a P.I. after all.

I suck at minding my own business.

"Mason," I said. "What else about your mother?"

Mason sighed. "Something's wrong with mom. This is a quote from her today: 'I want to know you're on your way to a full, rich life.' Like she was about to die or something. I'm going to find out what's really going on."

"How?"

"I'm going to find her doctor records to hack."

I winced. "I don't know, Mason, she might take offense."

He got up, tossed his empty soda can in the trash and opened the door. He looked back at me. "Maybe she expects it. She did name me *Huhatawuh Píta* after all."

He closed the door.

In Lupiti his name means "Digger."

So maybe she did.

I put away the maps and braced myself to call our new secret employee Judy Street and see what she's come up with since last night. Officially, she works for a dummy corporation called DRA — Demographic Research Associates. It explains all the research she does and hopefully keeps her off the radar of bad guys I'm after.

I sighed, anticipating the call. I really don't understand the woman, so I always feel at a disadvantage when dealing with her.

On the surface, Judy is the sweetest thing. She's got to be 50-something, although I'd never dare to ask. She's small, with pixie-cut grey hair that's always messy as though she just got out of bed — but artistically messy. She wears girlie clothes that show off a great figure and more makeup than I knew existed — and it all looks good on her.

She flirts with every man she meets, and they flirt back.

In sum, she looks like the kind of woman I should never, ever hire — a victim just waiting to happen for the dangerous men and situations I'm always getting into.

And yet... she has a fierceness to her. She helped us take down a very evil man in our last case.

And nobody can run our logistics like her. She saved my ass in Mexico a few months back by getting first a helicopter and then a private plane to me — faster than I thought possible.

I shook my head, still worried about what I was getting her into.

But... at least she was taking martial arts training. I wouldn't have hired her permanently without it.

# 6

## JUDY

Judy Street was curled up in her oversized chair, reading a romance novel, with Lola purring up a storm on her lap. Life just didn't get much better than this. She even felt virtuous. She'd spent all morning researching three Montana cities and familiarizing herself with websites that offered Montana jobs for high-quality carpenters, like Otto Hawking had been.

She looked over at her two new laptops sitting on her desk. They were each — Mason assured her — more secure than Fort Knox.

She lifted her five o'clock Glenfiddich on the rocks from her end table and closed her eyes as she took a sip. Something about how it felt sliding down her throat made it perfect.

Her eyes traveled over her apartment and she smiled. It was small — just a one-bedroom with a nook for her office. But it was downtown Tulsa, with a view and a balcony.

Although that balcony...

Six months ago, a man had climbed over it in the dead of night to kidnap her. If Sara hadn't been sitting outside in her truck watching, well...

Well, Sara had been.

The phone rang. It was Sara.

"You ready for this?" she asked.

"Girl, I was *born* ready. What d'ya need?"

"Get me to the Ratikuk Nation in Montana as early as you can tomorrow. And a hotel in Billings starting that same night in case I can move that fast. Dakota can't have that much time."

Judy filled her in with some of what she'd found. "Montana has 172 people missing right now, and 45 of them are indigenous people like Dakota. And I just sent y'all the employers for high-skill carpenters in Montana."

"Great," Sara said. "Get yourself to Big Sky tomorrow. Rent a two-bedroom townhome with an attached garage. Then check out the private house-cleaning company where Dakota worked. What was the name?"

"White Cleaning Services."

"Right. But don't try to get a job with them. I don't want anyone to be able to find you if everything goes to hell. Like it often does."

Judy smiled. "I just got myself some excellent fake I.D."

"Really? Where did you...?"

"I can't reveal my sources, or I'll lose my 'miracle worker' creds."

"Not with me — I still owe you for saving me in Mexico! How good are the I.D.'s?"

Judy smiled. "I've been assured they will pass any officer who stops me."

"Good work. You should tell Mason. He might..."

"He's already getting I.D.s for you, him and Connor."

"Always a step ahead of me. It's one of your most annoying qualities."

Judy laughed.

"Now don't get mad," Sara said, "but I worry about you protecting yourself on this case. You've only had six months to train in self-defense. Are you still a white belt?"

"Don't be silly. I stopped martial arts training after the first day."

"You what??"

Judy smiled to herself. She liked making Miss oh-so-in-control Sara — who hadn't wanted to hire her because she could get hurt — lose her cool.

"I'm not like you, Sara. I'm a tiny, 'mature' woman who is likely to get laughed at or — worse — break a bone if I try to punch someone. I'm going to use my feminine wiles instead."

There was silence on the phone.

Judy grinned.

Then she relented. "I'm kinda messing with you."

"You're giving me a blinding headache."

"I needed something different to defend myself. Something sneaky. Next time you see me, I'll show you my new hair pins. They're seven inches of stainless steel that can slide right into eyeballs or throats — like a greased pig."

Judy smiled at the silence. "And I have the cutest new necklace — it's a Pueblo turtle design. It fits perfectly in my hand with just a razor-sharp edge sticking out."

More silence on the phone.

"Well?" Judy asked.

"Can you use them? Under duress?"

"Yes. Connor's worked with me. I took all the SEPS courses on situational awareness. And Connor's spent hours and hours 'attacking' me and critiquing how I escape him."

More silence.

"Ask Connor if you don't believe me. He says I'm a natural, and he should know — with his Special Forces background."

"Okay, okay. You'll have to show me when we meet up. But meanwhile, Judy, you damn well protect yourself — however you have to. If you kill somebody who attacks you, I'll help you bury the body. But you will *not* make me go to your funeral."

Sara hung up on her.

*Well, dang,* Judy thought, rubbing moisture from her eye. *That's the sweetest thing she's ever said to me.*

# 7

## SARA

Bill Hanalho had arrived at the Ratikuk Reservation in eastern Montana a day before me and had met with people there, asking about Dakota and Otto — as well as representing the Lupiti people in meetings I wasn't invited to.

But one of the people he met with, Jackson Fights Alone, asked to meet me.

"He's heard stories of Joe White Wolf," Bill told me on the phone. "I told him Joe had touched you."

"Touched me?"

"It was the closest I could come up with. You're not Joe's heir, and yet you are in one way."

Bill was one of the three who knew I was a werewolf. I'd been forced to transform during that ceremony with his grandfather, and Bill had been there.

"That's a good way to put it," I said. "Joe actually did 'touch' me. It's how he passed it on to me."

I agreed to meet the two of them at 1:30 in the afternoon in Pryor, Montana, on the western side of the Crow reservation. Which confused me.

"Why on the Crow Reservation?" I asked. "Is that like neutral territory for your two different tribes?"

"I didn't ask why," was all Bill said.

It was a sunny afternoon, which helped ease the colder 35-degree temperature. Fortunately, there was no wind.

The sign said we were at Chief Plenty Coups State Park — which was a beautiful, green expanse with a strolling path along Pryor Creek.

Bill introduced me to Jackson, and the three of us started walking down one of the paths. Bill and I stayed on opposite sides of the man.

Nobody talked for a time, but my curiosity grew.

"So..." I asked. "When the two of you meet... is it like a rabbi and a priest meeting? Two people from two different worlds? Or is it more like a Lutheran and a Methodist — more similar?"

Bill's look was unreadable, but at least Jackson smiled. He said, "We see all religions as partners. The Crow say we're each a spoke in a wagon wheel that makes up the circle of life. The Ratikuk agree that people reach in their own way for the same creator."

I thought about it. "Your philosophy could eliminate religious wars. But I'm sure humanity would find other excuses."

Jackson looked at me. "You're cynical for one so young."

I nodded. "I've seen a lot." *Maybe too much.*

We walked along the Life Ways Trail, past the Chief's log cabin and a teepee. I tried to imagine having only that shelter to protect against Montana winters. I shivered.

Past the historic sweat lodge, we came to a bench that faced a sacred spring, and we sat. Again, Bill and I kept Jackson between us.

Jackson asked, "You knew Joe White Wolf well?"

"He was my nearest neighbor in the Colorado foothills for about five years. We often hiked and talked. But I don't know how well I really knew him."

"My grandfather met him. He told me White Wolf had a "presence" about him. Men watched him as they would watch a predator in the room."

He was quiet, giving me space to answer.

I kept my mouth shut.

"It was whispered to my grandfather that White Wolf could actually turn into a wolf. That he did so once to protect a child."

It was the question I'd expected, so I twisted my mouth and raised my eyebrows. "Well... he never showed it to me."

That was technically true. I'd never seen Joe as a wolf.

I smiled and added, "It would have been something to see."

I looked past him at Bill, to include him in my amusement, then turned back to Jackson. "He did have a wolf-dog named Skidi who followed him everywhere. When he died, she adopted me. Perhaps he had one in his younger days as well?"

Jackson didn't take my hint. Instead, he just stared at me. "You have very unusual eyes. There are tiny pinpricks of yellow sunlight in the brown."

*Oh shit.* That was the only noticeable change in my human form after my transformation.

I forced a smile. "Lucky me."

He opened his mouth to ask more, so I stared at him.

Since I turned, I've noticed women don't stare at men. Not unless they have a smile in their eyes. A direct stare is a challenge. But I'd answered all the questions about Joe I intended to. I stared at Jackson, letting him see the predator in my eyes.

His eyes crinkled as if he found me amusing. He nodded and got up. Bill and I joined him and we walked back towards the entrance, again, keeping Jackson in the middle.

When we reached the museum, Jackson turned to me. "I've told Bill what I know of both Otto's and Dakota's visits here and who they met — except for this. Because Otto was looking for work, I told him about a Jacy Hunter who lives in Hardin. Hunter has contacts in construction, including some rich-people builders. Some of our young men have found jobs through him."

We walked to the parking lot and our vehicles.

Jackson said, "I told Otto to be careful with this Jacy Hunter. He may be Native, but he's definitely not Ratikuk. There's a darkness in him."

Bill said, "Did you tell Dakota about him?"

"No. She was young and innocent, and there are too many disappeared Native women."

Jackson turned to me. "You two will both see him and be careful. And you will protect each other."

Bill and I looked at him, brows furrowed identically.

Jackson shook his head. "If I were blind, I could still 'see' you two."

He got in his truck and left.

Bill and I stood there, speechless.

Finally, Bill shook his head and pulled out his phone. "Let's go meet this guy."

Jacy Hunter wasn't interested in seeing us until we told him it was about a man Jackson Fights Alone had sent to him. Jackson's name got us an invitation to come on over. We took my rental car.

As I drove, Bill asked, "Have you met any natural wolves? Not just hybrids like Skidi?"

*Where was that coming from?*

"Just the one I rescued from that terrible Safari place in Texas. Why?"

"You're up here in spitting distance of Yellowstone Park. You might want to take a side trip to see wolves in their natural, wild state. Once the case is over, of course."

"Well... I've read everything I could find on wolves. All the research on them that's been published. All the books."

"Not the same as meeting them — don't you think?"

"You're right," I said, remembering the mental pictures I got from that wolf I'd rescued. And he'd spent his life in a zoo. How different would a natural, wild wolf be?

Hmmm...

# 8

## SARA

Jacy Hunter smiled like a shark — all wide and toothy — as he greeted Bill and me at his home in Hardin, Montana.

And yet the sides of his smile drooped down. It was as if his face were too tired to keep the smile up fully since he didn't really mean it.

He looked Native, but it wasn't from his face structure so much as the long hair — which had been recently dyed black. I knew because my wolf nose could still detect the faintly herbal scent of a hair-dye brand that targets men.

If Hunter was getting rich from construction referrals, he wasn't spending it on his house. The furnishings looked thrift store and out of date by about 40 years. His truck in the driveway stood out because it was new, but it wasn't ostentatious like some new truck models that would cost more than this house.

We sat down on chairs in the living room. Jacy did not offer us coffee or tea.

We introduced ourselves, Bill giving his full name and tribal connections. Jacy didn't reciprocate.

"Are you Ratikuk?" Bill asked, putting Jacy on the spot.

We got that fake smile again. "My family came from different tribes. I've got Ojibwe, Oneida, Meskwaki and Potatuck — and that's just the ones I was told about."

"All Eastern tribes."

Hunter nodded. "I feel more at home in the west. Don't you?"

Bill said, "Oklahoma has been my people's home for 150 years."

Jacy leaned back in his chair. "You wanted to see me about someone Jackson sent me? Someone looking for work?"

"Yes," I said. "His name was Otto Hawking. He was a master cabinet maker — very high-end. It would have been early March, 11 years ago."

"Eleven years? Are you kidding?"

"A high-end cabinet maker for custom houses. You can't get that many of those."

"I don't remember him, but what you describe... I would have given him two possible leads." He got up and walked to the kitchen and pulled out a pen and paper. He looked in his phone, wrote on the paper and came back to us.

"One of these two companies," he said, handing the paper to Bill.

"Surely you have records," I said. "Just check your referral fees for that time."

He froze for a split second, then said, "You're right." He tried on a rueful smile. "Except I lost all my records when the Big Horn flooded in 2019."

He turned to Bill, and the two men continued talking about flooding and droughts and the fertility of the land. All the stuff men talk about when they don't want to say anything but they're being sociable.

I tuned out and just watched Jacy's body language. It was a little stiff. He knew I was watching him, but he never once looked back at me.

Suddenly, both men stood and I realized we were finally getting out of there.

Jacy made a big deal of getting our coats for us; he even held mine up for me to slip into.

He looked at me as we left, saying, "A pleasure to meet you, Miss Flores."

Inside the car, I said, "Bill, drive us past some restaurants, will you? I'm hungry, but I want to see what our choices are."

Bill cocked his head at me, so I put my finger over my mouth. He drove us down the Main Street.

I opened all the pockets of my jacket and searched inside. Nothing. I took it off and used my fingers to squeeze all the fabric. I found the tracker inside the jacket lining, about the middle of my back. It was the size of a half dollar and attached with a very sticky tape. I pulled it off and set it on the car console.

We were driving past a place called the Milk Bucket Bakery & Cafe. "Stop here," I said, "and let me go look at the menu."

We pulled up, and I put my jacket back on. I touched Bill's jacket and motioned for him to take it off. I got out of the car and walked to the Cafe door. Then returned and got back in the car.

"It's closed," I said. "Let's try another place."

Bill pulled out while I searched his jacket. He had a tracker in one of his inside pockets, plus another inside a side seam. I removed them and gave him back the jacket.

We were past downtown now, and I saw a sign for La Cocinita. "Pull in here," I said. "Mexican food sounds good. Yes?"

"Good for me," he said.

I got out, motioning for him to stay. I took the three trackers with me. Inside were a bunch of hooks on the wall for jackets. The tables started three feet from the coats. I put my jacket up on a hook while dropping the pocket tracker into the outside pocket of the jacket next to me. I turned around to look at the room, leaning my back against the wall. Behind me, I slipped one of the sticky-tape trackers up under another jacket's liner.

I needed to get out of there fast before whoever was tracking us got to the restaurant. So I frowned, looked at my watch, picked my jacket back off the hook, and slipped the final sticky-tape tracker into a different coat.

I walked to Bill's door and motioned him to get out. "They may have put something on my rental car too."

He grinned. "Let me." He started feeling up the car, sliding his hands under it, especially right over where each wheel was.

"I think we're ok," he said, dusting off his hands.

# 9

## JUDY

Judy looked at the clock and fidgeted. She'd been kept waiting for almost an hour at White Cleaning Services, the Big Sky, Montana company where Dakota Hawking had worked for the past three months.

The deep chocolate leather chair was comfortable, but it faced a clock that seemed stuck — like it was broken and would forever show 2:06 PM. Until, suddenly, it showed 2:07. After another hour it might show 2:08. Maybe.

Three times she caught herself running her fingers over her Pueblo necklace — carefully keeping away from the razor-sharp edge. She had to stop. It would call unnecessary attention to it.

Addison Alden was the manager — Mason had found the name and texted her a picture of the woman. She looked almost like Jane Fonda, with the short, streaked-blond hair. But Alden had an extra 20 or 30 pounds on her.

When Judy arrived, the receptionist tried to block her, saying Ms. Alden was booked all day today. Judy insisted it was critical and that she would wait.

Now, 40 minutes later, Judy wondered how much longer they would leave her sitting here to express their displeasure.

A full hour later, the receptionist told her to go in the door at the end of the hall.

Addison Alden was shorter than she'd expected — she was about Judy's 5' 4" height, although her three-inch heels let her look down on Judy as they shook hands.

Addison greeted her with pursed lips and a frown between her eyebrows. She gave Judy one quick shake of hands, then sat down behind her desk.

"Miss Simpson," she said, using the name on Judy's fake ID.

"Ooh, I love your outfit," Judy cooed, honestly, hoping to break the ice. It was a turquoise jacket with a silk turquoise and navy scarf, with big gold nugget earrings.

Alden froze for a second and then said, 'Thank you.' She drummed her fingers on her Louis XIV knock-off desk, which had nothing on it except a rose in a vase, a sheet of stationery and a solid-gold pen. A laptop was on a side table.

"I'm sorry," Alden said, "but I have another meeting I have to get to. You said this was about Dakota Hawking?"

"Yes. Dakota is my goddaughter. She calls me several times a week, and I haven't heard a word since the fourth of January. Did she say anything to you?"

"No, she didn't show up for work, and we have been unable to reach her since. Young women can be very irresponsible. They meet a man and run off."

"Ooh, isn't that the truth? A sweet-talking man has been the downfall of many women, myself included. But that's nothing like my Dakota. She's always been almost *too* responsible."

"I'm sorry, but I haven't heard from her."

"Can you give me the name of a co-worker or two? I'm hoping to see if they might know something. Then I can get out of your hair."

"I'm sorry, but our staff is completely confidential. We clean houses for very wealthy customers who expect us to guard those names."

"I don't understand. I'm not asking about your clients — just a coworker or two she might have hung out with."

"That would be impossible. I'm sorry." Alden's hand moved under her desk, and the receptionist appeared in her doorway."

"Miss Simpson was just leaving," Alden said.

Judy stood. "Is there some reason y'all don't want me to find my goddaughter?"

Alden's head moved back as though she'd been slapped. "Don't be ridiculous. I have a business to run and girls with no sense of responsibility — like your niece — make it much tougher."

In the car, Judy reported the conversation to Mason. "The woman's a b-i-t-c-h. I hope you got into her computers?"

"I got into her tax records," Mason said, "but not anything that shows who works where. I suspect she keeps that on paper or a non-networked computer."

Mason had found 18 cleaning women employed by White for the past two months, including Dakota. One of them — Mariya Lysenko — had a phone number that Dakota had called twice while off work. Mariya was also signed up for the company carpool from Bozeman to Big Sky each day — the same carpool Dakota took.

Judy looked at her watch. She had just enough time to stop at the townhome she'd rented and check on Lola. She could feed her a treat and make sure she was comfy enough to not take revenge by tearing up a sofa.

Two hours later, right after sunset, Judy parked in front of Mariya Lysenko's tiny blue house jammed in between similar-sized houses in a low-rent part of Bozeman. The lease named Lysenko and her sister Yulia Babiak.

Judy shivered inside her new, lilac, down-filled coat that felt way too flimsy to hold back the 20-degree weather.

The woman who opened the door was in her 40s, with pale hair, a washed-out face, and eyes that looked battered.

Judy introduced herself as Dakota's godmother — who'd come here from Oklahoma because she was so desperate to find the girl. Mariya looked around to see if they were being watched, then pulled Judy in fast and closed the door.

"I liked Dakota — she was good to me when others weren't. I want to help her. But it must be a secret!

"A secret?"

"The company says to never, never discuss anything about our work. And to not discuss Dakota. We are told her name specific. I can't lose this job! It's the only health insurance we have..."

Mariya let out a deep breath and looked around like she might fall down.

"Girl," Judy said, taking her elbow. "You just sit down right now. Can I get you a glass of water?"

Mariya sat, but shook her head no.

"Hon, are you sick?" Judy asked, sitting across from her, taking her hand in hers.

Mariya sighed. "Not me. My son Danilo. He has tuberculosis and has to take four different drugs. Without the insurance, we couldn't pay for it."

Just then, a woman with remarkable family resemblance came down the stairs in full makeup, black pants, and a tight white blouse. It had to be the other name on the lease — Mariya's sister Yulia.

She frowned when she saw Judy.

The sisters got into a quick argument in another language — Mason had told her they were here on a visa from the Ukraine. The spat was about Judy, apparently, from the glares Yulia sent in her direction.

The argument ended, but without resolution as Yulia got in Judy's face and said, "You cost Mariya this job and you kill Danilo. You understand?"

Judy raised her hands in surrender. "I understand."

Yulia stared at her for several seconds. Then she nodded. And left.

"Sorry," Mariya said, sitting back down. "She must be here in the day for Danilo, so she works at bar — only night job she could get. My job is from seven in morning to six at night — counting travel in the van. So much time away. But I have the health insurance."

"Do you have any idea what happened to Dakota?"

"No. Last week she just stopped showing up."

"Was Dakota ever afraid? Did she think she was in danger?"

"She said nothing like that."

"Did she seem worried about anything? Say anything to you?"

Mariya shook her head. "No. And I would have noticed."

"Did she ever act different than normal? Surprise you, even a little?"

Mariya again shook her head no, then she reconsidered. "Well... the last day I saw her. When we rode home in the van... Usually, she talks to me. Makes little jokes. But that day, no. She just stared out the window, but... not like she's looking at anything. Like she was thinking."

"Do you know what houses she cleaned that day?"

Mariya shook her head. "We weren't in the same crew."

"Did crews stick together? Do the same houses? Or did y'all move around?"

"Usually same crew and same houses. So we know exactly what the owners want. They can be very... they have many requirements."

"Do you know who else was on her crew?"

"No... yes! A girl named Willa... no Willow. Dakota went out with her a couple of nights. She said Willow goes out all the time to bars and dancing."

"Anyone else?"

"Our crews are three people, one of whom is the crew boss. But I don't know who was boss for her crew."

"One last question," said Judy. "Did Dakota have a boyfriend?"

"I don't think a serious one. But she went dancing sometimes. He was named Miguel... let me think... Miguel Rios."

At the door, Judy hugged her. "Thank you so much. We won't say anything, and you shouldn't either. Just know — you may have saved Dakota's life."

# 10

## SARA

I dropped Bill back on the rez at the Ratikuk Lodge. I wanted to make sure nobody was waiting to attack him in his room, so I walked with him to the door.

And, yes, that's my story and I'm sticking to it.

When I opened his door, none of the faint people smells in there were strong enough for someone to be waiting inside. I turned to go.

"Sara..." he said. "Should we talk?"

*Oh, hell no.*

Bravely I turned around to face him. "We already did. You have a life planned out. So do I. They're just different."

*My god, the man looked good.*

"But..."

I raised a hand to fend him off, a little panicked. "I can't get distracted now. We have so little time to find Dakota."

I shook my head and started down the hall. Then I turned back. "Watch out for yourself. Jacy had two trackers on you. Get home and stay safe."

He said nothing, just looked at me with sad eyes. Or, at least I wanted them to be sad.

I left.

In the car I checked the GPS. It was about an hour-and-a-half drive to Billings. Maybe I could cool off by then. I slammed my steering wheel. "Damn him!"

What was wrong with him? If he wanted to *talk*, he could have done that three days ago. Or three months ago. Not in the middle of a case where I needed — hello! — to be alert and thinking about the case. Not about him.

My watch said it was 11:30 P.M. — the middle of the day for Mason. I called him, desperate for the distraction. And I wanted him to dig into those two companies Jacy had given us. The names he said he would have given to Otto.

Over the phone I heard, "Hello?"

I frowned. Mason didn't do hellos. Mason usually started right in talking about whatever he'd just dug up on the case.

"Mason?"

"Yes?" he said. "What is it?"

"Mason? What's wrong?"

"I see. It sounds urgent. Yes. I'll get right on it." He hung up.

Was he in trouble?

Then my brain registered the background sounds of dance music and people partying and remembered Mason's promise to his mother. He was on a date with one of the girls.

I shook my head. Poor Mason. His date was going bad enough for him to use my call to end it.

Twenty minutes later, my phone started blaring the Police's "Every Breath You Take." It was Mason's joke "stalker" song that he'd programmed into my phone to announce when he was calling me. I'd deleted it once, but somehow he got it back on. Now, I even liked it — although hell would freeze over before I admitted it to him.

I grinned.

"What do you need?" he asked.

"Sounds like Lupiti Girl number one was not a winner?"

"Yuck it up. I just spent two excruciating hours I'll never get back again."

"Don't blame me!" I gave him the two construction company names.

I exited the Ratikuk Reservation and turned left at Hardin, onto the old U.S. 87, towards I-90 and Billings.

Mason said, "I've scraped over 5,000 photos from the most recent Ratikuk Native Days, and they're running through my facial recognition software looking for Dakota. Then I'll look at those photos to find anyone who is looking at her. And I'll search for more photos of that person."

"Maybe," I said, "also flag anyone who shows up anywhere in a photo of Dakota more than once? Even if they're not looking at her?"

Mason was silent for a minute. My headlights showed the exit for the Big Horn County Airport. I had about 10 miles until I'd hit I-90.

Mason said, "Good idea. It'll add a little time, and we'll get a bunch of false positives, but we're less likely to miss someone."

"We still can, though, right? If he was smart enough to stay farther away from her so he wouldn't fit in the same camera shots."

"Hey," Mason said, "if it was easy, you wouldn't need me."

I grinned.

"I talked to Judy," he said. "She gave me all the custom-house construction companies in Montana and Wyoming. I'm going to see which were also around 11 years ago and match them against the two companies you just gave me from Jacy."

"Did you talk to Connor?"

Connor Rockwood was the fourth member of our little team, also newly hired. Connor was a former Special Forces man who transitioned to executive bodyguard.

He was also a workaholic. A month after our last job ended, he took a temp bodyguard position. "Tell me when you get the next job," he'd said, "but I can't sit around waiting."

I wondered how that affected his relationship with Lillian, a former client of ours and a friend of mine. When he was in Tulsa, he lived with her and worked at her shooting range business.

She had to know he was even more of an adrenalin junkie than I was.

Mason said, "I got a message from him. He's trying to find a replacement to take over his bodyguard job so he can join us."

A sign flew past, telling me Interstate 90 was two miles ahead.

I saw movement in my side mirror. Something dark.

A vehicle with no lights on!

It slammed into me.

My car went flying off the road at 60 miles an hour, bouncing over rocks and scrubby bushes. Two telephone poles flew past — one close enough to reach out and touch.

I was still going fast when the ground suddenly dipped down.

I saw a big rock just before I hit it and flew forward in my seat.

Airbags attacked me as I felt the car flip over.

Then I noticed nothing.

# 11

## SARA

Growling woke me up — plus snarling and the sound of very big teeth snapping together.

The world was upside down.

Something was binding me — trapping me.

I struggled harder, and then I saw the source of the noise.

It was me.

I could see the very long end of my nose — my snout — as my jaws grabbed another section of seat belt and snapped and ripped it to shreds.

The seat belt separated and I fell down onto the roof of the car. I was in an upside-down car in the middle of blackness lit only by stars and a partial moon.

And yet, looking through a hole a giant must have punched in the windshield, I could see clearly the dirt, rocks, and scrubby plants outside. No sign of human habitation.

Inside the car I could see my reddish grey fur and my four paws.

I grinned.

Yes, that was stupid.

I remembered being hit by a vehicle with no lights and being knocked off the highway.

I was in trouble.

But I'd *transformed with no pain!* I wanted to dance in happiness. I knew intense pain or shock could cause me to transform, but this was the first time the entire agonizing, bone-breaking transformation happened while I was unconscious. Maybe...

I smelled a man.

My grin disappeared, and my nose turned into the breeze coming in the shattered passenger window.

Two men.

If I tried to open the mangled car door, I would make noise. It might also be futile.

I put my front paws on the grab bar, now under the passenger side windshield, and gauged the hole was big enough. I jumped through the opening, bending my paws as I landed, going for maximum quiet.

Did they have night-vision or thermal goggles?

If so, I needed to stay right up against the heated car engine to help blur my signature.

My ears told me the men were coming from the rear of my car, so I put it between us and waited.

There's something primal about hunting or being hunted. Something foreign to the timid me I was before. There's the adrenalin and the exquisite sense of being alive in the moment.

My heart pounded, my lungs grabbed more oxygen, and my whole body tingled.

I also felt it in human form, but as a wolf it was... overwhelming. Intoxicating.

I felt more alive because I was dancing with the alternative.

They were closer now. Maybe 40 feet away.

I was grateful to be downwind of the men so I could smell them but they couldn't smell me.

Their odors separated. They moved to surround the car.

One was a young man, a smoker, who had just eaten a hamburger with... ketchup. My tongue licked out. The meat odor tantalized, although I'd skip the ketchup. I realized I was hungry.

The other man was older and I could smell sugar on his sweat. He was diabetic. And... he had a whiff of fear-sweat stink.

Interesting.

Why would he be afraid?

I could smell gun oil from both their directions, so they were armed.

Why would an older — presumably more experienced — bad guy be afraid of going after a lone female in a wrecked car? Especially when there were two of them, and both were armed?

Did he know something about me?

He stopped.

The smoker kept coming.

I went down in a four-legged squat beside the front hood of the car, my stomach almost touching the dirt.

I saw him now. Big guy. High, slow steps like he was trying to be sneaky but he wasn't used to it. He moved towards the side of the car.

I squinted. Damn my mediocre wolf eyesight but I couldn't see... no, wait, I could. No night-vision goggles on him.

He got close to the car and then moved his pistol in a full circle — seeking anyone nearby. He squatted down and stuck first his pistol then his head into the car window. Looking for me.

I smiled — the car now blocked both him and me from the older guy's view.

Keeping low I crept forward, around the headlight, my paws digging into the earth.

He started to back out of the window and I opened my jaws.

His neck stuck out. I leapt and took the offering. One strong bite and a twist and it nearly came off.

Because I crunched his voice box, he never yelled. The only noise was a thud as his body hit the side of the car.

I was about to spit out the chunk of flesh in my mouth when I got an idea. A stupid idea but, hey, I'm known for those.

A way to get some answers.

I swallowed, setting off my transformation back to human. A minute later — a painful, painful minute later — I was a naked, helpless-looking female.

Quickly, I rubbed some of the still-oozing man's blood over my lower body — keeping it far away from my mouth area.

I was still worried about why the older man stank of fear.

Then I let myself fall down on my back about five feet away from what was left of the man's body.

I closed my eyes.

Yes — it was the hardest thing I'd done thus far.

The older guy approached very slowly. Almost reluctantly.

I knew the second he saw his partner's nearly severed head because I heard a gasp. I heard panting sounds — he was hyperventilating.

From his smell, he was maybe 20-25 feet from me. I could hear his heart pumping hard and fast.

He didn't come any closer.

I heard, "Who... who are you?"

I laid there, silent.

"Who the hell are you?" His voice cracked.

I said nothing.

"Lady, you got two choices. Either sit up and talk to me, or I'm going to shoot you and get the hell out of here."

Well... if those were my choices....

I slowly brought my hands to my head and moaned. "What happened?"

I glanced at him and let my eyes go wide at the rifle he had pointed at me.

"Who are you?" I asked.

He shook his head, impatient with me. "What were you doing with Jackson Fights Alone?"

"Huh?"

"Don't lie!" He reached inside his jacket and pulled out a picture and waived it at me. It was a picture of me, Bill and Jackson from early this morning at Chief Plenty Coups Park.

He said, "I know you met him."

He shoved the picture back in his jacket, his body shaking in agitation.

He mumbled, "Never would have taken this job if I'd seen that picture first."

"Huh?" I repeated.

"Did he do this?" He pointed at the dead man.

*Jackson? What was he talking about?*

"I knew he could command eagles. He made one pluck an eye out of a man who... well, never mind. But I didn't know about other animals. Did he protect you?"

I frowned at him and shook my head.

"When you met with him. Did he offer you protection?" His face had turned red and his voice got louder.

I raised my hands, showing I didn't have a clue what he was talking about.

He yelled at me. "Why didn't his animal attack you too? Are you protected?"

Ah... I nodded slowly.

"Jackson gave me a blessing," I lied.

A quick thought made me add, "Me and the man with me. He gave us both a blessing."

He nodded. Then he spun around 360 — looking out into the night. "Is it still here? Whatever did this to Jerry? A wolf?"

I looked around too. "I don't know. I was unconscious. I didn't see what it was."

"Great. Just great." He looked at me. "I'm supposed to make sure you're dead. Make it look like an accident."

I raised my eyebrows at him. "You think that would be smart? I mean... look at him." I tilted my head, pointing it at the dead man.

"And why are you naked?" He looked shocked, as though he'd just noticed. "Get something on."

*He just noticed??*

It was totally inappropriate, but I was irritated. Mad even. *What was I — chopped liver?*

"Sure." I gritted my teeth and looked inside the car.

I saw my phone lying on the roof, near my bag. I quickly picked it and and saw the call with Mason was still open. I tapped "007" quickly and laid it back down. It was the sign I gave Mason when I wanted him to listen but stay silent.

He'd probably already guessed that because he hadn't been yelling over the phone for me to pick up.

And, yes, the code was silly. But with this job I took my giggles where I could get them.

I pulled out my bag and put on the first sweater and jeans my hands touched. And my backup Nikes.

"So," I asked. "Who wants me dead?"

The man was shaking his head. He mumbled as if talking to himself. "Maybe I could shoot you and get away in time."

I looked out into the blackness. "The wolf would know."

He grimaced. "There's no way now to make it look like you died in the crash."

I shook my head. "Nope."

"But I have to. They'll kill me if you get away."

"What's your name?"

"Davy Brown."

"Davy," I said, putting sorrow and certainty in my voice. "They'll kill you anyway, even if you did the job right. They'll want no loose ends."

He didn't look surprised at my words. He must have come to the same conclusion.

He sighed.

"I have an idea." I started walking to him. "Do you have someplace you can go? At least two states away from here?"

He nodded, but he wasn't sure.

I continued towards him.

"Can you get rid of the car you're driving? Quickly?"

He nodded, surer this time.

I stood before him.

He shook his head. "They'll find me."

"If you tell me what you know about this, I'll give you Jackson's blessing. It will help you."

He frowned at me.

"Watch." I extended my right hand towards his eyes. I stopped it about a foot from his face and willed my index finger, from tip to the knuckle, to change to a wolf claw surrounded by wolf fur.

His eyes grew huge.

Slowly I moved the claw until I tapped it — once — on his forehead. Then I pulled back my hand and slowly let the claw turn back into a finger.

"Tell me everything," I said.

He complied.

# 12

## MASON

**M**ason hung up the phone and rubbed his eyes. He leaned back in Sara's office chair and sighed in relief.

Sara was alive, not dead in the road. And she had a new lead from one of the goons who crashed her car.

The damn woman was going to give him a heart attack.

How many times had it happened?

He's talking to Sara on the phone, then BAM! — crash sounds. Then silence. Then minutes and minutes of not knowing if she's dead or unconscious. Or fighting for her life. Or maybe just sitting there contemplating her navel while he's left in the dark.

Enough times for them to need a signal — the "oo7" she entered into her phone. To tell him she's gone James Bond on him and he needs to remain silent.

He twisted his mouth.

*Well, at least it got me out of that date with Aponi.*

What was his mom thinking? The girl didn't have a single thought in her head that wasn't about clothes or babies. And she talked about them nonstop. He had nothing in common with her. Nothing to talk about.

Which reminded him...

He got up from Sara's office chair and opened the mini-fridge.

Sara always kept some diet lemon-lime soda in it for him. He popped the top, gulped down a chug, and sat back down.

He'd found his mom's doctor by checking out her recent bank transactions. Then he'd set up an app to break into her doctor's medical-center files.

He checked the app and nodded. He was in.

He found his mom's file and started reading. Minutes later, he was still staring at the file when his phone startled him.

He shook his head to clear it.

"Hi, Connor," he said. "The bodyguard business is too boring for you after working with us?"

"The client was a new level of asshole even for CEO assholes. I was glad to pass him off to someone else. Are you sure you got some action here? A girl missing for a week doesn't sound like much."

"Two goons just ran Sara off the road for meddling."

"Fantastic! Well... that is... I assume she's okay? But that means..."

Mason tuned out of the conversation as his eyes moved back to his computer — to his mom's file.

"Mason!" Connor's voice was loud in his ear.

"What?"

"Is Sara OK? Does she need help?"

Mason shook his head. "No, one goon's dead and the other just told her everything he knows..."

Mason trailed off, his eyes glued to his computer.

"Mason!"

"What?"

"You keep zoning out. You drunk or falling asleep on me?"

"Sorry," Mason said. "Some stuff has come up I have to deal with. Get to Bozeman, Montana, and talk to Judy. Between the two of you, you'll know how to get what you want from the construction companies Otto worked at. Talk to you later."

Mason hung up.

His phone rang again.

*Not now!*

Mason looked at it. It was his mom.

*Oh boy.*

"Hi Mom."

"Mason, ditching a girl after two hours is not giving her a chance."

"*You* spend two hours with her! How can one woman talk that much and not say a single thing that's interesting? And how could you do this to me? Do you hate me?"

"Of course not... Alright, I had my doubts about her... but she's stunningly beautiful."

"Beautiful is great for hooking up, Mom. When I marry, it'll be to someone whose mouth I don't want to tape shut."

"Okay, I'm sorry. You'll like the other two girls much better."

"I hope so. And one more thing, Mom. When were you going to tell me about the thyroid cancer?"

The phone was silent.

Finally she said, "Who told you?"

"I hacked your doctor's records. Like you knew I'd do."

"My *Huhatawuh Píta*," his mom said, her voice turning soft. "How did I know that was your perfect name?"

"The cancer, Mom."

"Oh, don't worry about it. My doctor assures me there's a 90% survival rate for women."

"For five years? What about 10?"

"Well... that's still 85%. It's nothing to worry about. I'll be fine."

"If you were sure of that, you wouldn't be trying to marry me off."

"Oh, Mason. Yes, that factored in. But I also worry about you being lonely. You're so self-sufficient — but we all need someone. Don't think this lets you off your promise to try out the other two girls."

"If the next one I try is as bad as the first, I'm skipping the final one."

"Don't worry. You'll like the next two. Got to run. Love you."

The phone disconnected.

"Love you too, Mom," Mason said to the dial tone.

# 13

## SARA

It was eight in the morning, Montana time, when the four of us connected via Mason's secure phones. I was in Billings, Judy and Connor in Big Sky, and Mason was in Tulsa — where the lucky dog got an extra hour of sleep because Tulsa time was an hour later.

I said, "Let's start with where we are on Dakota. Mason — any luck yet on facial recognition from all the Native Days photos?"

The phones were silent.

"Mason?" I asked.

"Sorry," I heard. "My apps are still running. So far I've got eight men and four women she interacted with — two of whom look like vendors — and another seven pictures of men just looking at her. And there are four other men who appear near her in two or more pictures. That's 21 people, with more to come."

"Get them to Bill Hanalho," I told him. "He can send them to Jackson Fights Alone. Tell Bill we need to know names and two-sentence bios as quickly as possible. Anyone he flags you need to check out."

I thought for a minute. "Especially flag anyone Jackson doesn't know."

"Judy?" I asked. "What about Dakota's contacts in Montana?"

She said, "Addison Alden was Dakota's boss and she's a real piece of work. She stonewalled me and I don't know if it's because she's dirty in this or if she's just protecting her company.

"We found a coworker of Dakota's who said she was unusually quiet or worried after her last day of work. To find out what houses she worked on, we need to find a coworker named Willow, no last name. The girl is known to hang around evenings in Big Sky because she likes to dance. Dakota joined her sometimes.

"Our source also said Dakota had a hot boyfriend named Miguel Rios. She didn't think it was anything too serious, but... police shows on TV say you should always check the spouse or the lover."

"Good job," I said. "Mason, would it be crazy to try to find Instagram and TikTok photos posted of partying in Big Sky during our time frame?"

The phones were silent again.

"Mason?"

*What was going on? I knew nine A.M. was the middle of the night for Mason — but he'd never been this out of it before on day calls.*

"Sorry, what?" he said.

I said, "We're trying to find Dakota's coworker Willow — who loves to go dancing in Big Sky."

Mason: "I'd have better luck if I knew the top places where the young and poor go dancing in Big Sky. Then I could tap into their surveillance footage."

Judy: "I'll make some rounds tonight and get back to you. I'll also ask if anyone knows Willow."

I said, "Okay, that's Dakota. Let's switch to Otto, and I'll go first. Otto met with Jacy Hunter in Harding, Montana. Jacy finds construction jobs in the area for local men. He says he gave Otto two company names — Rocky Mountain and Wall & Sons. From his paychecks, we know Otto also worked for Bierhals, a company that Jacy didn't mention.

"This gives us three construction companies to look at — hard. And, because somebody tried to kill me last night — construction is looking like one of our best bets. Connor? Judy? How do you want to handle it?"

Connor said, "Judy and I were just planning that. She's going to be overt and I'll be covert."

Judy: "I'm already known as Dakota's godmother — I used that with the cleaning companies. I'll just use that same line to talk to the places where Otto worked. Places Dakota probably went."

Connor: "Judy will wrap them around her little finger, and we'll have a better shot at getting names of people Otto worked with."

Judy: "Then Connor can make buddy-buddy with any of the names we get."

I nodded. It was a good plan. "That's our best lead right now."

"So what will *you* be doing?" Judy asked. Yep, that was Judy.

"I'm going to go talk to the man who sent goons to kill me last night."

# 14

## JUDY

Judy pulled up to Bierhals Custom Homes, the second company she'd visited this morning. This was the company Otto had pay stubs from, but which had *not* been mentioned by Jacy Hunter.

She checked herself in the rearview mirror and touched up her coral lipstick. She mussed her silver — not grey! — hair and told herself she looked good.

"Show time," she said as she got out of the rental.

The building had a brick front and a flat roof (In Montana? Were they crazy?). It was a skinny 50 feet wide, but it was very, very long.

She pulled her lilac puff jacket tightly around her. It was a tiny bit warmer than yesterday, but she hated, hated this cold. And it was windy! Between the cold and the wind, her eyes were watering. Good thing her mascara and eyeliner were extra waterproof.

The Internet told her Bierhals was run by three middle-aged male partners, each with a different specialty. The partner Judy wanted supervised the actual building of the houses and the the high-end subcontractors they hired. His name was Ezra Hendriks.

An older couple was already in the reception area, looking at architectural drawings on the walls while waiting. They were probably here to design a custom home, if Judy read the cost of their clothes correct. They were dressed casual, but their jeans were designer and the woman was wearing cowboy boots from Tres Outlaw — which cost her at least $2,500. Maybe a lot more. The man's watch looked like a $107,000 Radiomir Panerai.

One of the partners — the sales guy — came out and ushered the couple back through the door to the offices.

Judy moved closer to the log-burning fireplace and warmed her hands.

Finally, Hendriks came through the door. Judy walked to him, hand outstretched. They shook.

"Thank you so much for your time Mr. Hendriks," she said as they walked to his office. "I promise I won't take much of it."

He offered her something to drink.

"Anything warm," Judy said. "How do you stand this weather? It's cold enough to freeze the teats off a frog!"

Hendriks laughed. "Where are you from?"

"Tulsa. Our idea of a blizzard is a quarter inch of snow that makes us all too terrified to drive."

He smiled.

Judy pulled a picture from her purse. "This is my goddaughter, Dakota Hawking. She's the daughter of one of your past employees — Otto Hawking. She's disappeared, and I'm trying to find her. Did she come to see you recently?"

Hendriks looked at the picture and shook his head. "No, I haven't seen her."

He handed the photo back and leaned back in his chair. "Otto Hawking's daughter. Damn but I miss that man. He did the best custom cabinet work I've ever seen."

He frowned. "But Otto... I heard he..."

"Yes, he died in Yellowstone Park eleven years ago. And that's the problem. Dakota didn't want to believe his death was an accident. So right after she turned 18, she came up here to find everyone who knew him. And four months after that, she goes missing."

"I'm sorry to hear that. How can I help?"

"Dakota was looking for friends of her father. Work friends. Play friends. Anyone he would have hung out with while he was up here. But I don't know who she found to talk to."

Judy took out a hankie and pressed it to her eyes.

"I'm worried about her, Mr. Hendriks. She's called me every Saturday at noon for the past five years — except last Saturday. She's not answering her phone and she hasn't shown up to work. I'm hoping you can give me the names of some men he worked with up here. Maybe also men he hung out with."

"Have you called the police?"

"Of course. But I don't think they're looking that hard. She's 18 and been gone a week. They think she's flighty, but I can assure you she is not."

Judy used the hankie again. "Can you let me know who he worked with? Or was friends with? Or drinking buddies?"

"Of course." He opened his laptop then wrote down some names and phone numbers on a paper and handed it to her. "The first guy, Gus Torres, was his closest friend here. The two below are the men he worked with the most."

Judy pocketed the paper. "Thank you so much. I'll let you know what we find."

Judy expected him to rise and show her out. But Hendriks just sat there, his eyes unfocused. Thinking.

Judy sat there in silence for a few minutes. When he still didn't say or do anything, she said quietly, "There's something else you think I should know, isn't there."

His eyes returned to her. "Yes..."

He trailed off.

Then she saw him decide to continue. "Have you talked to his lady friend?"

Judy's eyes went wide. "As in 'girlfriend'?"

Hendriks nodded.

"No, but I'm pretty sure I should."

Hendriks nodded again. He went back to his computer and wrote down another name and phone number and passed it to Judy.

He said, "If Dakota didn't already find Lydia... don't tell her about the woman."

"You're a kind man, Mr. Hendriks."

# 15

## SARA

I saw a fat Jeep Grand Wagoneer — with the grille that looks like a mouth full of braces — come out of the parking lot for the Montana Energy Review Board. I used my small binoculars to verify the license plate.

Yep, this was the one Mason told me is owned by Gabal Crowley — a man I intended to talk to before the night is over. Mostly about hiring two men to run me off the road and kill me.

I wondered how antsy he must be, given one of those men was found dead this morning instead of me, and his other man disappeared.

I followed his Jeep on streets for ten minutes, then followed him into a public parking garage in downtown Billings. He drove around in rising circles until he ended up on the roof.

I drove past him and parked between him and the elevator.

I patted my pockets, a nervous tic before any encounter, making sure my guns, my knife, and my zip ties were all with me.

I sat there, wondering if he was secretly meeting someone here in the parking lot. But after sitting in the SUV for a couple of minutes, he opened the door and started towards the exit.

He was alone.

I opened my car door and stepped out as he came near.

"Gabal Crowley," I said. "Why did you want me dead?"

His eyes opened wider and his right hand moved to his chest, but he didn't pull the pistol he obviously had holstered under his left arm. Instead he looked carefully around us. He looked for a bigger threat than a woman with empty hands and no weapons showing. Not seeing anyone else, he lowered his hand.

"I don't know who you are."

Wow, he was a terrible liar. I didn't even need to smell him to know. His shifting eyes spoke volumes.

"Really? Davy Brown and his buddy said you hired them to run me off the road and make sure it killed me."

"I don't know what you're talking about," he said in a louder voice.

I smiled and walked closer to him. "I'm not recording you, idiot. If I was, I surely wouldn't mention how *not* sorry I am that one of your goons got his head half bit off."

"Yeah? Where's that Indian friend of yours?" He kept looking around, sure I wasn't so stupid as to be alone.

"Which one?"

"The one from Oklahoma. Like you."

"Gone back home. I needed him for an introduction. Now I don't need him anymore."

I *really* wanted them to forget about Bill.

He said, "What do you want?"

"Why would my asking about Otto Hawking make you want to kill me?"

"Why are you here?"

"Why did you disappear his daughter, Dakota Hawking?"

"I haven't disappeared anyone," he said, again in a louder voice. "Is that why you're here? To make false accusations?"

Interesting. He was not lying when he said he hadn't disappeared anyone. But he did recognize her name.

"I'm here to figure out why you — or more likely your boss — doesn't want any questions about Dakota."

He smiled. "Well... why don't you come back to my place and we'll talk about it."

I smiled. "What an excellent idea! Your car or mine?"

"Mine is bigger."

"Of course it is."

We walked back to his car and he tried to get me in the back seat, which I refused. He hesitated at the entrance to the freeway.

"I know where you live," I said.

"My family's there." He pulled to the side of the street and stopped.

"And you don't want them to see me, in case I disappear too?"

He shifted in his seat and frowned. He didn't like me talking about being disappeared as though I thought it was funny.

"I don't mix business and personal," he said.

I grinned. "That seems a little sanctimonious for a political 'fixer.'"

His hands clenched on the steering wheel.

Suddenly, it wasn't fun anymore. I asked, "Do you know if there are any traffic cams here?"

He frowned and then looked around. "I don't think so."

"Not good enough." I pulled out a phone and hit autodial for Mason.

"Yes?" he answered, puzzled at the phone because he'd been in my ear and listening since I first accosted Crowley — a fact I had no intention of sharing.

"I'm parked on North 29th Street in Billings, Montana, halfway between Second and Third Avenues North," I said. "Let me know if there are any webcams that could be covering me."

I turned to Crowley and said, "It won't take long."

He pulled out his cell and called someone as well. "George, I'm going to be delayed an hour or two." He listened for a minute. "Can't be helped. I'll let you know if there's a further delay."

We watched each other for a minute or two before Mason said, "Okay."

"I'm putting you on speaker," I said, then tapped the button on my phone.

Mason said, "There's one possible camera that would take me longer to investigate. But if you drive up to Sixth Avenue, turn right, and stop in the middle of the block, you'll be at a guaranteed camera-free zone in front of the library."

"Thanks," I said, hanging up. I waived my hand at Crowley. "Shall we?"

He drove the three blocks and pulled over, put the car in park, but left it running.

We turned to each other.

"Well?" I ask.

He shook his head, "Ladies first, I insist."

So his goal in talking to me was to find out what I already knew. Okay. I decided to give him a taste.

"As I'm sure you know, I'm a private investigator hired to find Dakota Hawking. Since she came up here trying to find out what really happened to her dad, I also need to look into Otto Hawking to find who she might have talked to. I've got some leads. But I might never have considered your boss until you made this move. Why does Al Rasmussen want me dead?"

He flinched when I named his employer, but then something relaxed in him. As if what I knew was bad but not, all things considered, terrible.

"Nobody wants you dead," he growled.

I laughed. "Liar."

He took a breath and plastered a smile on his face. "Lady, you've been watching too many movies or TV shows. I do some security work for a number of people..."

I rolled my eyes at him and whipped out my phone again. In the photo app, I found the picture Mason sent me of Crowley with Rasmussen. I showed it to him.

"Yes, I do some work for Rasmussen. And several other people."

"So how did Otto Hawking come into contact with you? And don't say you don't know him." I found a picture of Otto and showed it to him.

He looked me in the eye and said, "I've never seen this man before."

He lied much better this time. I might have believed him except for the faint, almost-undetectable stink of fear that my wolf nose recognized.

I shook my head at him. "More lies."

I exhaled. "You know, most people have to get to know me a little before they try to kill me. You were too quick. It was stupid — either plain stupid or arrogant stupid. You sped up my making a connection between Otto, Dakota and your boss. Hell, I might never have made it."

He looked away and mumbled. "That's not what we hear."

"Not what you hear?"

How did they hear about me? I haven't been in the papers. Except... well... my firm was mentioned in some of the news about uncovering the sex trafficking ring run by a billionaire casino owner.

Horrified, I looked at Crowley. "Your boss was involved with Winston Bainbridge? He bought sex-trafficked women?"

"No! Absolutely not. We just heard it was your P.I. firm that uncovered him. It meant you were good at finding people."

I was relieved to smell he told the truth on this.

I saw him decide his next move.

He'd learned what I knew. It was time to finish what he'd started.

His hand was half way to his gun when I grabbed it, jerking three of his fingers back so far they snapped.

He started to scream, which lifted his head slightly — exposing his left carotid artery perfectly for my strike. I'd gotten pretty good at this blow, hitting hard enough to drop him but not hard enough to kill him.

The noise stopped mid-scream, and he collapsed against the side of his car.

I looked at him and I knew with certainty that I should kill him. And I also knew I wouldn't.

I was certain I'd regret it because he would come for me again.

Pissed at myself, I shoved his limp body over into the passenger seat, switching places with him, and secured his hands and feet with zip ties. I fished out his cell phone, stuck his right thumb on it and unlocked it.

"Mason," I said.

"Here."

"I'm calling you with his cell phone so you can hack it and then wipe it." I dialed him.

"Got it," I heard. "Leave it on."

I put the phone in a cup holder where it wouldn't get bumped and started up the Wagoneer.

Crowley came awake as I was driving back to the parking lot where my car was. I saw movement out of the side of my eye and glanced at him. I raised a finger in warning.

"Right now I'm planning to return you to the garage alive. You say one word or make one move and I'll happily change my mind and kill you. Like I know I should."

I saw him carefully test his bindings and realize they were secure. He nodded once and relaxed.

A flash of rage tore though me.

I realized I'd been hoping he'd try something so I could justify killing him.

*A man in my situation wouldn't hesitate*, I told myself.

Then I wondered if that was true.

Maybe, when this case was over, I'd ask Connor.

# 16

## CONNOR

Connor Rockwood scanned the stereotypically blue-collar bar. It had a sign emphasizing the cheap beer, and it had sawdust on the floor to soak up toppled drinks and the occasional blood spilled from a fight. There was even a pool table.

But these patrons looked further down the economic ladder — they were sitting apart from each other and serious about their drinking.

The man Connor came here for was sitting in a booth near the back. Alone.

Judy had given him three names of men who had worked with Otto at Bierhals Custom Homes. He'd talked to two of them this afternoon, and they both suggested he talk to Jerry Katz — a man who hated Otto Hawking's guts. One of them told Connor that Otto and Katz had fought over how Katz was treating a woman.

They both agreed fists got involved.

Connor could see it. Katz had slicked-back hair and a flannel shirt hanging open over a wife-beater tank top.

He was reported to be a regular at this bar.

"You Jerry Katz?" Connor asked.

"Who wants to know?"

"Your new best friend. Can I buy you a drink?"

Katz looked him over.

Connor hunched his shoulders and bent his knees, trying to make himself look less like the man he was — a big, strong, former Special Forces guy who was still in great shape for a man in his 40s. His 6' 4" height all by itself made many men defensive.

His looks got him all the bodyguard jobs he wanted, but he had to work to look like an ordinary guy you'd shoot the shit with.

Katz tilted his head, then said, "Sure, why not?"

Connor caught the bartender's eye and ordered two of what Jerry was already drinking.

Katz slugged down the drink he was nursing and started sipping the new drink.

Connor tasted his and hid the grimace. It was barely a step up from rotgut. It tasted like the stuff he'd inhaled to get drunk at Bagram AFB after a harrowing mission. He could still taste the puke that often followed it.

He pushed it away.

He said, "I'm tracking down all the people who knew Otto Hawking, but I can't get a read on the guy. Some people tell me he was a straight-up guy. Others say he was an asshole."

"He was an asshole. But I heard he was dead. Is he alive?"

"No, he died 11 years ago. But they're considering naming some building for him. So I'm supposed to make sure they won't regret it."

"Huh."

"Tell me everything you can remember about the guy and I'll keep you lubricated. Hey, you want any food? They got anything here?"

Fifteen minutes later they had hamburgers and fries sitting in front of them.

*I'm getting soft,* Connor thought, staring at the grease running off the burger. Ten years ago he would have torn into it. Now... he lost his appetite.

"The guy was an asshole," Katz said again, his mouth full of half-chewed hamburger.

"How'd you meet?"

"A bunch of us used to hang out at Rossy's Bar after work. One of the regulars brought him, and he kept coming."

"Construction guys? Or?"

"Yeah, most of us were in the skilled trades. Carpentry. Masonry."

"I don't know the field. Do you work exclusively for one builder? Or hire out by house project for anyone?"

"Some was exclusive. Most of us hired by the job."

"And Hawking?"

"Yeah?"

"What projects was he working on?"

"Why do you..."

"Just some boxes I have to fill in for my report. For background."

"Well...we both worked on a couple of houses up in Big Sky. One was for some tech millionaire. Hawking did their kitchen cabinets. And he did the kitchen and library at a big ranch in the Shining Peak Club."

"Was Hawking ever involved in anything shady? I'm hearing organized crime is involved in stealing heavy construction machinery here in Montana. They sell it to contractors trying to cut corners?"

"Might have been, I don't know. "

"What was the beef between you two?"

"The asshole tried to get between me and my woman. Butting his nose in where it didn't belong."

"There was some talk he might have been killed instead of it being an accident. You ever hear of him getting sideways with any tough guys here?"

"Naw, although I wouldn't be surprised. I'm not the only guy who don't like assholes."

## 17

---

## JUDY

Judy had trouble finding Otto Hawking's woman friend — Lydia Taylor. She was no longer at the phone number Judy had been given. In fact, she'd moved five times and changed her phone six times in the 11 years since Otto died.

But Mason found her.

Lydia Taylor was working for three different online companies, writing content for food and decorating blogs. Which meant she didn't leave to go to work. Her home turned out to be a tiny house in a new community of them, all painted in cheerful greens, purples and yellows.

Judy just hoped they were warm.

It was 16 degrees outside when she left her Big Sky townhome rental. She'd left an extra treat for her cat Lola — just to thank her again for not needing outside walks like a dog would.

Now, at 10 A.M. and the lower altitude of Four Corners, she suspected it was still under 20 degrees. She shivered inside her big, gorgeous puff coat.

*Maybe she should buy another one two sizes bigger and wear it over this coat?*

Judy liked Lydia on sight. "Oh, my gawd, I love your hair," were the first words out of her mouth as she looked in awe at Lydia's wild mop of red, uncontrolled curls.

Lydia laughed. "Well, I like yours too — all mussed like you just got out of bed. And you're brave enough to not dye it. I'm too scared to go grey."

"Girl, if my hair looked like yours, I wouldn't change a thing about it." Then Judy shook her head. "I'm sorry. You must think me an airhead not to introduce myself. I'm Judy Street, and I'm hoping you're Lydia Taylor."

Lydia's smile faded and her brows moved closer together. "Yes?"

"I need your help to find a missing girl. Could I come in? I'm freezing my fanny off out here. And your house is leaking heat."

"Okay...."

"I've never been in a tiny home before. Do you mind if I look a little? Why you've got a good sized kitchen, don't you? And as much office space as I have in my one-bedroom apartment in Tulsa."

"You said a missing girl?"

Judy pulled out a Last Chance Investigations card and handed it to her. "Otto Hawking's 18-year-old daughter has gone missing — a week and a half now. She came up here fixin' to find out what really happened to her daddy. She doesn't think his death was an accident."

Lydia sank down on the home's only sofa. "Otto. It's been years."

Judy sat down next to her. "I just talked to his former boss here and he said Otto was completely taken by you. Said he got a big smile just saying your name."

Judy saw tears well in Lydia's eyes.

"Oh, hon." Judy patted Lydia's leg.

"I knew it was wrong — that he was married. But he'd left there and moved here. What kind of marriage is that?" She looked at Judy.

"Girl, the heart doesn't much care what's right and wrong. It wants what it wants."

"His daughter? He loved her. She thinks he was murdered? And she's now missing?"

Judy nodded.

"Do *you* think he was murdered? Your company?" Lydia looked at the business card. "This 'Last Chance Investigations'?"

"Let me ask you one question, Lydia. Did Otto use drugs? Fentanyl?"

Lydia sat up straight. "Hell no. And I would know. He worked all day and was with me all night. He wouldn't even touch alcohol except for beer. He got me to throw away a good bottle of vodka I had in the house. He said he'd seen too much of what it could do."

Lydia frowned. "Did someone say he was using drugs?"

"His body had fentanyl in it."

"It killed him?"

"It and the freezing weather."

"Then someone did murder him."

Lydia looked at Judy. "How big is your company?"

Judy shook her head. "I don't understand. We have four investigators. Why are you asking?"

"If someone powerful with unlimited money came after you, could you handle it?"

Judy nodded. "I see. Did you hear about the rich casino guy in Houston who was selling women."

"About five months ago? I was so glad they caught him and rescued those girls."

"We took them down. Look." Judy pulled out her phone and found the one article that mentioned the scheme all fell apart when Last Chance Investigations was hired to find one of the missing women. She showed it to Lydia.

"Do you have lots of money?"

Judy frowned. "We have all we need — no matter who we go after."

"Then I have something to give you. I don't know if it will help, but... You have to promise you'll tell nobody it came from me."

"I'll tell the two owners of the company but nobody else. We are champions at keeping secrets."

"Wait here."

Lydia climbed the ladder at one end of the tiny house to the loft above. Then she came down with a manilla envelop, plain except for Lydia's name on the front.

"This was sealed in a separate envelope sent to me by an attorney in Billings. Otto had paid him to wait 30 days, in the event Otto died, before sending it."

Judy held out her hand, but Lydia held the envelope tightly to her chest. "I'm afraid I'm endangering you by giving you this. Somebody searched my house a week after he died. Really tore it up searching. Otto was smart to delay it coming to me."

"We're the right people to give it to."

Lydia shook her head, unsure. "He'd want me to help his daughter no matter the risk. But I still feel bad about giving it to you."

She handed Judy the envelope.

Inside was a single page. The handwriting was terrible but Judy could read it.

> Conversation overheard on Jan. 6, 2013 at 475 Lodgepole Pine Rd., Big Sky, MT, between a man I knew to be Sigurd Rasmussen, a rich local cattleman, and a younger man — both guests at the house:
>
> Young man: "You're crazy. You'll cost us millions!"
> Rasmussen: "It's my money."
> Young man: "But…"
> Rasmussen: "Not another word. You won't change my mind."
>
> The young man was later identified by me as Al Rasmussen, Sigurd's son.
>
> Signed by me, Otto Hawking, on January 16, one week after Sigurd Rasmussen's death by 'natural causes.'

Judy frowned and looked at Lydia.

"Otto was different after that man's death. Quiet. It was the only time I saw him afraid."

"Do you know which job he was on when he overheard this?"

"Not for sure. Most of his work the last two months was on a ranch in that fancy Shining Peak Club. He never knew who the owner was — just some corporation."

Judy put the paper inside a pocket in her coat, not in her handbag.

"I need to get back to work," Lydia said, looking at her desk.

Judy nodded and bundled back up.

"Remember, you didn't get anything from me."

"I only asked you about Dakota's disappearance. It's too bad you didn't know anything about it."

At the door, before she opened it, Lydia grabbed Judy and hugged her.

"Listen to me," she said in Judy's ear. "You get yourself a gun and you watch out. Otto always warned me to never get between a rich man and his money."

Lydia scrunched up her face. "Oh god. I guess he didn't listen to his own advice." A tear ran down her cheek.

Judy hugged her. "Thank you for the warning."

# 18

## SARA

I moved inside a large tool cabinet in the garage, cramming myself next to a garage vac and a long-handled broom. I wore black jeans, a black jacket, and a black ski mask pulled over my head.

Judy was expected back in 15 minutes to this townhouse she'd rented in Big Sky, Montana.

Connor knew what I was going to do, and he told me I was an idiot. He said Judy could defend herself.

I told him I'd believe it when I saw it.

Judy was doing great for us. She fit the team as if she'd always done this kind of work. But I was still distracted by worries about her. In our last case, two men knocked her out and were carrying her away to be tortured for information. If I hadn't been there to save her...

Now this case was turning deadly. We'd stirred up everyone and kicked over a lot of rocks.

This was when the snakes came out.

I wanted very much to take her off the case and send her packing back home.

The garage door started to open, so I closed the cabinet door leaving just a slit of visibility. She drove in slowly, and once her headlights moved past the cabinet, I exited and headed around the back of her car.

It felt funny lurking right in view of her rear camera, but as long as she didn't put the car in reverse, I'd be okay.

She turned off the car and opened the door.

As she stepped out, I rushed up and grabbed her by the throat — jerking her out of the car.

She grabbed weakly at my arms.

I *knew* she couldn't handle this!

To my shock, there was a sharp, terrible pain in my left arm — and I lost the grip.

I stared stupidly at her. She grabbed her necklace and swung it towards my throat. Because I knew it had a razor-sharp blade, I grabbed her left arm, using my full strength to halt her attack.

Her right hand came forward and she reached inside the cuff of the arm I was holding. She pulled out something that looked like a nine-inch nail with twists in the shank and plunged it towards my neck.

I grabbed that arm too.

So that's what she struck me with!

Her arms were trapped, so she swung her pointed boots up into me — right where my balls would be if I were a man.

Even without balls, it hurt like a sonofagun.

I was so proud of her that I wanted to pull her in and hug her.

She kicked down on my kneecap, hard enough to crack it if my improved reflexes hadn't jerked my knee back. Even so, I felt blinding pain and my knee buckled.

"Judy," I said. "It's Sara. Stop fighting."

She kicked for the other knee. I realized she wasn't listening.

I lifted her by her arms and shook her.

"Judy!" I yelled. "It's Sara. Stop!"

"Sara?" She sounded dubious. "Take off the mask."

"I have to let go of your arms to do that. Will you promise not to stab me again when I let go?"

"Maybe."

I laughed.

She sounded really pissed. *As I would be*, I thought.

I put her down and removed my mask.

She glared at me for the longest time.

"I needed to know you could protect yourself," I said, sounding as defensive as I felt.

"Don't expect any sympathy for your injuries."

"Can I see those 'hat-pin' weapons of yours?"

She rolled her eyes, turned on her heels, and headed for the door inside.

"You were really good," I called after her. "I'm very impressed."

"You can kiss my Oklahoma butt."

She slammed the door.

I grinned. She could hold her own if one man tried to grab her. But, faced with guns... I should ask Connor how good she was with her handgun.

As I limped into the townhome after her, holding my wrist to stop the bleeding, I made a note to myself to trust Connor's evaluations in the future.

# 19

## SARA

I had camped out in Judy's second bedroom, waiting for my knee and wrist to heal.

I also pondered why I was so protective of her. The look she gave me today said I'd taken my concerns too far. It's just... I worried about her differently than how I worried about Mason or Connor.

A nightmare I occasionally have flashed in my eyes. My mother was in trouble, and I was running to rescue her. But no matter how fast I ran, I never could reach her.

It's not real. My mother died in a hit-and-run car accident while I was at school. Did... did I want to protect Judy because I couldn't protect my mother? That was a crazy idea.

And one I should *never* mention to Judy.

Connor poked his head into the room, telling me pizza had arrived for lunch.

He kept trying to squelch a grin as he looked at me, then gave it up and let it spread across his entire face.

"How's she doing?" I asked him.

"Oh, you're on her shit list. I wouldn't turn my back on her any time soon."

"And?"

He nodded. "She's feeling pretty impressed with herself, going over and over what you did and what she did. She should be impressed."

"She should," I agreed. "How's her shooting?"

"Not as good. She keeps anticipating the recoil and it hurts her aim. I had to move her down to a .22 before she could hit anything."

"A .22 won't stop…"

"I got her hollow-point bullets. As her aim improves, they'll do the trick."

"Thank you, Connor. Your training is likely to save her life one of these days."

He nodded, his grin completely gone. "It's why I pushed her so hard."

"But," I said, "What if *two* men with guns come for her?"

"You remember those panic transmitters we got for her on the last case?"

"The ones she wore in her bra?"

Connor grinned. "Yeah, those."

"She almost got killed because she took her bra off to sleep."

"I added a transmitter to that necklace she wears. She's promised to wear one or the other at all times."

"It'll alert me if she pushes it?"

"You, me and Mason. She's as safe as we can get her."

"Good." I looked at my watch and got up. We walked to the kitchen to demolish the pizza.

Judy ignored me at first, but she kept looking at my bandaged wrist.

"Did I hurt you?" she asked, frowning. "I mean, you deserved it if I did, but…"

"Don't worry," I told her. "I lucked out. You missed nerves and the major blood vessels. But even with me being lucky, you broke my grip on you. So good job!"

"But I didn't beat you, did I?"

"It wasn't a fair test because I knew about your necklace. When I saw it coming at me, I jumped back as fast as I could. A bad guy trying to grab you wouldn't have that knowledge. Wouldn't even suspect it."

"Really?"

"That necklace would have worked on me for sure."

She smiled.

I smiled. "And that kick to the balls would have worked too, except..."

"Except you don't have them."

I laughed. "Exactly. Now could I see how you're carrying those hat-pin nail things?"

She pulled back her sleeves to show wrist sweatbands — like you use when playing tennis — holding them against her inner arms. The weapons themselves were beautiful in a deadly way. Forged stainless steel, each about nine inches long — one straight and two with a cork-screw twist on them.

I thought about getting some for myself, but decided claws were just as good, and I didn't have to remember to wear them.

The three of us were all meeting secretly at Judy's rented townhouse to have a case update and figure out where to go from here. So after lunch we called Mason and he did whatever he does to make sure the call couldn't be hacked.

I suggested Connor go first.

"There's some talk about large-scale, organized-crime theft in construction here. Otto Hawking quit working for one of the companies and was in some kind of beef with the local contractor's union. But the unions here in Montana don't have much power compared to other states. And I've found no signs that Dakota looked into it. I'm not sure if I should continue on this."

I said, "Let's see what else we have. I'm writing off Dakota's boyfriend Miguel. They went dancing a couple of times, had sex once, and then she just lost interest. He called her a few times, but they never got together again. He's already been through two more women since then. He doesn't know anything about her investigation or where she is. And, yes, I'm sure of it."

I turned to Judy and handed her a paper. "Miguel knew Willow's address. Can you follow up and find out what houses she and Dakota were cleaning?"

She nodded.

"Mason?" I asked.

"First one warning," he said on speakerphone. "The forecast says you're getting a blizzard there around six or seven tonight. For you Tulsa natives, that does not mean a half-inch. It means eight to ten inches. You might even be snowed in tomorrow — so plan accordingly."

"That's so sweet of you, hon," Judy said. "Or it would be if we couldn't hear you gloating. What's the weather there? Still in the 50s?"

"Hitting 51 today, thanks for asking."

Mason added, "I've got the Ratikuk Native Days photos all sorted. There was one man who stood out. I'm sending his picture to your phones. This guy's name is James Marley. He's a public relations assistant to Alfred G. Rasmussen — who is a prime target. Right, Sara?"

"Yes," I said, "given that one of his fixers, Gabal Crowley, hired two men to run me off the road and kill me."

"Rasmussen," Mason filled us in, "is on the Montana Energy Review Board. It's made up of ranchers and oilmen and Rasmussen is one of the ranchers. He owns 154,000 acres in Montana. He's rich and he's powerful."

"My turn?" asked Judy.

I nodded. She handed each of us in the room a copy of Otto Hawking's handwritten note. She asked Mason, "Did you get the copy I texted you?"

"Got it," he said.

Judy said, "Y'all should know Otto died three days after he wrote the letter.

"I spent last night researching what Sigurd's death meant financially to his son. The quick answer was Al inherited $600 million, most of that from 100,000 acres of land.

"What took me longer is checking out a later article in the *Billings Gazette* that said Sigurd had been planning to put most of those acres in a 'conservation easement.' It's a hot new tool to protect the land. If Sigurd had signed it, no development or commercial enterprise could ever go on the land — even if it was sold."

"No mining?" I asked.

"Nope. It would have prevented almost any increase in profits Al could get from the land. And if he sold it, he'd get only a tiny fraction of what he could sell it for now without the easement. Because the new owners also couldn't develop or commercialize it."

"Anything else?" I asked and got no takers.

"Okay," I decided. "Mason, get everything you can on both Rasmussen personally and this Board he's on. Finances, decisions they've made, and decisions they might make in the future.

"Judy, get me everything social about Al. His wife, kids, mistresses. What causes are they involved in? And look into the other members of this board. Their spouses. Their charity work. Their kids.

"Mason, expand your search to the other Board members too — their finances. And who are they allied with professionally?

"Judy — who do all these people hang out with socially? Like that Supreme Court judge... do they have special rich friends or cliques they belong to?"

"When I get everyone's info, I'll pay a call on Rasmussen."

I turned to Connor. "I've got a tough assignment for you. Rasmussen has to be involved in Otto's murder, but there's no evidence Dakota even knew he existed. Her disappearance may not be tied to him. So what got her disappeared? I'm worried we're missing something."

"Coincidence? Maybe she just ran into a serial killer."

I tilted my head at him.

"Yeah, I know. Not likely. You're asking because you think the answer may be in his construction jobs?"

"Let's run with the last two houses that Dakota cleaned. When Judy gets you them, see if either of them matches the house Otto mentions in the note he wrote. It's the only remaining lead we have for her."

Connor nodded. "I'll let you know."

I'd grabbed my stuff and was heading for the garage when I heard a cat hiss like she was ready to kill something. I turned and saw Judy's cat Lola on the back of a sofa, back arched to the sky, fur standing on end so she looked twice her size, and fangs bared.

A man laughed.

I turned to see Connor with a big grin. "Judy said she had to lock Lola in a room when you're around, but I wanted to see. Boy does she hate you! What'd you do to her?"

I used Mason's trick and scratched my cheek with my middle finger. I muttered "men" and "overgrown boys" and slammed the door on my way out.

It would have been funny, except when you have a secret as big as mine, it's hard to laugh at any tell-tale signs that show.

# 20

## CONNOR

"I'm an idiot to join up with you guys," Connor said to Mason over the phone.

It was four hours after the meeting.

"I just created a spreadsheet. A fuckin' *spreadsheet*! Do you know the kind of crap my buddies would heap on me if they found out?"

"Now, now," Mason said soothingly. "I won't tell a soul and you won't, so they'll never find out."

"And now what? Couldn't I just go shoot everyone on it? Nothing serious — just wing them to get them to talk?"

"Are you asking me for help — while pretending you're not?"

*Shit.* "I guess I am."

"Talk to me."

"Judy talked to Willow, so we now know the two houses Dakota cleaned on her last day at work. One of them is that Lodgepole Sanctuary house where Otto overheard the Rasmussens."

"Excellent!"

"The problem is that Al Rasmussen hasn't been to that house in the past four months. So he couldn't have interacted with Dakota.

"So... in case he isn't the connection with her, my spreadsheet lists 23 construction people who worked on that house. I could investigate each of them, but... I think we'd be fishing in the wrong pond."

"Because...?"

"They're not big enough. Not powerful enough. Not for something that's lasted 11 years."

"How about people who stayed in the home... isn't Judy working on that?"

"She says it's coming real slow. And... I think that's a dead end, too. The chances of the same guest being there 11 years ago when Otto worked there and also on the last day Dakota was there..."

"You think it's the house owners?"

"There's something subtle in this whole setup, Mason. It's Machiavellian even. I think there's some puppet master behind the scenes."

The phone was silent, and then Mason said, "I think you've got better P.I. instincts than you think."

"You agree? But that leaves us nowhere. You said they can't be found."

"I said I hadn't found them yet. They're buried under some of the best secrecy you can buy. I've tracked them down four levels only to find a fifth one under that."

Connor: "So what now? Maybe... maybe there's another way. Let's think like some asshole CEO bad guy. Why would you buy a home and then jump through all these hoops to make damn sure nobody could find out you owned it? Would you do all of that just to hide from taxes?"

Mason said, "Corporations and the rich will do a lot to hide from taxes, but... no. I don't think that's it. Because two people went missing."

"Maybe they have hidden cameras and recording equipment. And they invite CEOs and politicians to be house guests — in order to find blackmail material?"

Silence.

"Mason?"

"I'm thinking. I hadn't considered that. If that's the scheme, it would be too risky to have someone physically monitoring the recordings. The video would have to be sent automatically. And electronically. Which means I can find out. I'll jump on this and let you know."

"Don't hang up yet," Connor said. "In case that isn't it, I can think of one other reason for this level of secrecy — to hide your identity so you can set up secret meetings nobody will find out about. You could pretend to be a guest yourself and just blend in with the other hot-shot guests."

Silence.

Mason: "But how would we find out which guest it was — out of hundreds?"

"You wouldn't do all this for one meeting a year. We need to find out who's there frequently."

"Agreed," said Mason. "This is a better assignment for Judy. Get her on this. I'll let you know when I've checked out the blackmail recordings angle."

"So... I can dump the spreadsheet, right?"

Mason laughed and hung up.

# 21

## SARA

It was one P.M. when I left Judy's. I needed to be in Gardiner, Montana, on the northern border of Yellowstone Park, as quickly as I could. Driving would have required 121 miles going a ridiculous north then east route before turning south. It would have taken over two hours.

Fortunately, I'd reserved a helicopter. Flying directly southeast took just 40 miles and 14 minutes.

Mason was well burrowed into Al Rasmussen's computer systems, so we knew Al was coming here this afternoon.

A small amount of lithium had been found in the mountains about 15 miles to the east of Gardiner, deep in the forest. Rasmussen and another Montana Energy Review Board member were flying out to see it. Lithium is the new holy grail for mining operations because it's needed for lithium-ion batteries, which power so much of our electronics.

"Guess what lithium is found in?" Mason asked.

I rolled my eyes.

"Don't roll your eyes," he said, although he didn't have a visual on me. At least I didn't think so.

"You'll like this. The bodies of the rock where you can find it are called "Hellroaring Plutons.""

"Mason," I pleaded. "Just tell me where, when and how many people are likely to be with him."

"Okay, if you want to wallow in ignorance. I was just trying to help."

"Maybe I should ask you how your dates are going?"

"Rasmussen is taking a helicopter from the Gardiner airport at three thirty. He'll have another Board member with him, at least one or two security, plus the pilots."

"Thank you."

"How are you getting out there? There aren't any roads."

"I'm thinking about buying a horse. That snowstorm isn't supposed to hit until six or seven tonight, which leaves plenty of time to get there and back."

"A horse?"

"I know how to ride. I did it when I lived in Colorado."

"Have you been on one since you left there?"

"No, but why would that... oh." I hadn't been on a horse since I was transformed.

"Judy's cat hates your guts. Horses are close to deer or elk, so I'd bet they won't like you either."

"Guess I'd better find out."

Fifteen minutes later, horseless, I left my car on the outskirts of the town and hiked into the forest where nobody would see my transformation. I'd brought my adapted backpack which carries my clothes when I'm on four legs.

I started running well north of the Yellowstone River, needing the tree cover. Soon I was zipping through the trees on four paws, my biggest worry being assholes with guns who like to lurk on the outskirts of Yellowstone Park for the chance to shoot any wolf who steps across the invisible line marking the park boundary. As long as they didn't go north into the woods, I was probably safe. The trees kept me hidden.

I laughed, remembering my attempt in town to make friends with a horse.

I'd found two of them tied up to a local camping supplier. I walked up to them, saying, "Ooh, what beautiful horses." They got one sniff of me, and their eyes bugged out and they backed away as far as the reins would let them. When I kept moving towards them, they reared and probably would have broken their ties.

Lesson learned. My horse-riding days were over.

I estimated it would take two hours to get to the lithium discovery site.

I clipped a GPS finder to the outside of my backpack because I wasn't sure if I could trust research. I'd read dogs and wolves (and birds) have what's called Cry-1 in the cones in their eyes. It's sensitive to the magnetic compass and is what allows birds to fly long distances and reliably end up in the same location.

I oriented myself in the direction I wanted to go. I planned to run using only my senses, then stop in a half hour and see if I was really where I should be.

But I chickened out.

After what I thought was 20 minutes, I stopped to check. It was actually 30 minutes, but I was — amazingly — going the right direction. Sonofagun!

I checked again after another similar time. Again in the right direction.

How was I doing it? I had no idea. I just headed the way that "felt right."

I knew when I'd arrived. There was a clearing large enough to land a helicopter. And some Mini-Cooper-sized equipment for digging, which they probably had to hang from a chopper to bring in here. There were also two large tents hidden under tree cover, most likely to keep them from aerial view. It all looked temporary and testing-phase, not the full-blown operation that was likely to come.

I found a memorable rock about 100 feet outside the site perimeter where I could stash my backpack.

I laid out my shoes and socks right next to where I would transform. Bare human feet are not meant to walk in forests. At least not *my* bare human feet, which are sissies who wince at anything they step on which isn't flat ground.

My teeth were happy to rip open freeze-dried, wild-caught salmon packages, which I scarfed down. Then I lay on my tummy and swore very bad words as the transformation back to human took me.

I indulged myself afterwards by lying still for a couple of minutes, marveling in gratitude at the lack of pain in each of my body parts.

*My jaws — no pain! Fantastic!*

*My knees — no pain! Fantastic!*

Then I got up and opened the backpack. I dressed, thankful winter down coats can be squished down to a small size that can fit in the bag and still leave room for boots, socks, and more clothes.

I took my GPS from where it was clipped to the backpack and pocketed it. I put a tiny earpiece into my ear and added an earring that doubled as a transmitter.

"Hi Mason," I said. "I'm at the site and ready."

I put a button on my collar that said "Save the Wolves!" And then checked with Mason to be sure the camera behind the button was working.

Mason told me it was 3:30 Mountain Time, so I had 15 minutes before the helicopter would arrive.

"How's your mother? How was date number two?"

Mason sighed. Loudly.

"Another loser?"

"No... she was okay. At least she could carry on a conversation."

I laughed. "Pretty low bar there."

Mason was silent.

"So... she could talk, but...."

"But she's going into social work."

"So?"

"I must be a bad person," he said. "I just don't want to hear all the terrible things some people are going through. It makes me feel guilty that I'm not also going into social work. And the stories are so horribly, horribly depressing that I could never do it."

"Most people couldn't do that job — me included. But you do a lot, Mason. You've set up a scholarship program that provides free college for your tribe. And you're helping me save lives."

"It doesn't feel like enough."

"It never does. But we each have our own gifts. She couldn't have rescued those women who'd been sold as sex slaves. She couldn't take down the whole damn network, so they couldn't hurt anyone else. But you could. And you did."

He was silent.

"Look on the bright side," I said. "You've only got one more woman to go and you're free!"

My ears picked up an unnatural noise coming from the West.

"Helicopter coming," I said, then moved back behind a tree about 200 yards away from the clearing. Hiding.

When the windstorm from the rotors stopped, I peeked and saw four people step out, leaving one pilot behind. There was one older executive type, a female whose deference said she was an assistant, a guy who could only be a bodyguard, and Rasmussen. As I'd seen in his picture, Al Rasmussen was in his late 30s with a scrubbed, Middle-America look. You'd peg him as a lifetime middle manager, someone who would never rise higher.

He did not look like a man who'd kill his daddy for money. But I've learned it's smarter to judge a book by its cover than a man by his.

I was surprised Gabal Crowley wasn't the bodyguard who showed up. I expected him here because I thought he was Rasmussen's regular bodyguard.

Men who try to kill me are not usually still around to worry me — and I regretted leaving him alive in Billings two nights ago.

I'd make sure Mason got a good picture of this one through my button camera.

I let the four of them walk into a tent. When they came out, I moved into view and strolled towards them, my empty hands clearly visible.

"Hi, guys," I said.

Four pairs of eyes opened wide at seeing me. Rasmussen's were especially wide and, from the glance he stole at the bodyguard, I knew he recognized me.

The bodyguard's hand went inside his jacket. But it stayed there. For now.

"Where did you come from?" asked the other board member.

I faced him directly so Mason's camera could get a good image for identification.

"I rode a horse out here. I need five minutes to talk with Mr. Rasmussen; he's been ignoring my calls."

Rasmussen froze at my words. His eyes moved to the other board member then back to his bodyguard. I could see he wanted to sic the man on me. But a harmless-looking woman... how would that look to the other guy?

"Honestly," I said, "no more than five minutes. Then I'll leave and you all can get back to whatever you're doing here."

The other guy turned to Rasmussen and said, "Al?"

"Give us five," Rasmussen said, then took my elbow — surprisingly gentle — and he and the bodyguard walked me out of earshot of the other two.

I looked at the helicopter, but the pilot had his nose in an ebook.

When we were far enough away, I removed my arm from his grasp.

Rasmussen looked at his watch. "Five minutes. What do you want?"

I laughed. "What do I want? I want to know how it feels to have killed your father so he wouldn't lower the value of the land you inherited from him. I want to know if your last goon I met, Gabal Crowley, is still alive or if you've had him killed. And — hey — might as well throw in that I want world peace too."

I moved closer to him and looked in his eyes. "But I'd settle for knowing where the hell Dakota Hawking is."

His face had gone beet red. His eyes darted to the pilot and the others, as though making sure they couldn't have heard this. Then he turned to the bodyguard and I couldn't read the expression between the two.

"Dakota Hawking," I reminded him.

"I don't know who she is."

I inhaled through my nose, searching. And there it was — those tiny stink molecules wafting from his body that told me he was lying.

"Liar. *Where* is she?"

His eyes narrowed and he spread his hands out, palms up, "I have no idea where she is."

I inhaled again and those little stink molecules were drifting away. Dissipating.

I cocked my head. "That's the truth, isn't it? You don't know where she is."

He pulled back, looking surprised.

"Who has her?" I asked.

"I don't know that either," he said, regaining his composure.

I frowned. This time he was giving off mixed signals. "You don't know who has her, but... You know who took her?"

"No."

"Now you're lying. Let me be clear," I said. "We can make a deal. You get her released within 24 hours, and I'll forget all the evidence connecting you to your dad's murder. Otherwise..."

I turned my back on him and walked towards the others. I nodded at the woman and then at the man. "Sorry to have taken your time," I told them. "Guess I'd better start back if I'm to miss the snowstorm they say is coming."

I turned and walked back to where they first saw me, grabbed my backpack, and continued on into the forest. Supposedly going for my non-existent horse.

I walked for about a quarter mile, then found a nice log to sit on.

"So..." I asked Mason. "Did you find out who the other board member was?"

Through my earpiece I heard, "It's Tyler Patel. He's the chemist member of Montana's Energy Review Board."

"And the new bodyguard?"

"Still running him through facial recognition."

"Let's think this out," I said. "Rasmussen knows who took Dakota but he doesn't know where she is or who has her. That means he's not running the show. There's somebody bigger and more powerful out there, which fits with Rasmussen's aging frat-boy manner. He's no mastermind."

We were both silent.

"And why isn't she dead?" I asked. "I mean... she could be. But why didn't they kill her immediately, stage it as a mugging, and let her body be found? It would have been much simpler for them."

In the distance, I heard the helicopter start up. I listened, but it didn't rise immediately.

My ears pricked up. Someone was walking in the forest. Coming towards me.

In my ear I heard, "Maybe they need her for a bargaining chip? No, that doesn't track. Maybe... maybe they only needed her to disappear for a short time?"

"Interesting idea," I said to Mason, keeping my voice soft and my eyes where the steps were coming from.

"Miss?" A man's voice called out. "Miss?"

"Someone's here," I whispered to Mason. I stood up.

The bodyguard came into view. "Oh, there you are! I was afraid I wouldn't catch you. Mr. Rasmussen gave me a note to give you."

He held out a folded paper and walked towards me.

Something seemed wrong.

His left hand held the paper. But before, when he'd reached in his jacket...

He was 20 feet from me when I saw his right hand extend, pistol in it, pointing right at me. I raised my hands because he couldn't... not with witnesses...

*Oh hell.* They wouldn't hear a thing with the helicopter engine running.

The gun fired.

*Oh shit! Oh shit!*

It was pointed at my head! The one place I was afraid would be fatal.

Everything really does slow down when you're facing possible death. I saw that bullet coming for my head as if it were in slow motion.

My body jerked away at that same, slow-as-molasses speed even though I used every ounce of strength I had to jump aside.

I could see it was going to hit me.

Maybe it will be fine, I prayed. Maybe I'll just transform and I'll be healed. All good. Just like a bullet hitting me anywhere else.

Maybe. Maybe.

But... I'd never taken one in the head before. Maybe this would kill me?

I didn't want to leave Mason. Or Connor. Or Judy.

And then there was Bill. What could we have had together?

And Skidi. I *couldn't* leave Skidi.

The bullet was relentless. On and on it came. I'd moved only slightly in all this time. Instead of the middle of my forehead, it hit my left temple.

It jerked me backward, and then I fell onto the earth. I landed hard.

I smelled the top layer of fresh leaves and pine cones fly up and then come back down to rest with me. I scented the rot of the old leaves underneath them. Under me.

I felt my heart beating in my chest, but that was all I felt.

My hands, my legs — they might as well have disappeared in a poof. Like they never existed.

A blurred, dark image came and stood over me. I saw a gun point at my heart from four feet away.

It fired.

Then I saw nothing.

# 22

## JUDY

Judy poured herself another cup of coffee and brought the mug and her MacBook Air to the comfortable chaise in her rented Big Sky townhouse. Outside this window, she could get a glimpse of skiers on one of the trails. The loud colors on their clothes made them look like small hot-air balloons floating by on the wind.

She smiled.

Her cat Lola jumped in her lap and started purring. She picked her up under her front paws, kissed her on the nose, then quickly extended her arms so Lola's swipe at her face missed.

"I'm just too quick for you, sweetie," she told the cat.

Sitting Lola down at the foot of the chaise, she pulled over her laptop.

"So... where was I?"

She opened her most recently saved Numbers program and nodded with satisfaction at all the entries in it — given she'd only started it yesterday after the meeting.

Between then and now, she'd worked 14 hours — with still more to do.

The house in question was located inside the ultra-exclusive

Shining Peak Club at Big Sky. It was a one-mile drive from the club's exclusive ski slope and three miles from the public Big Sky ski lifts.

It was a two-house compound that backed up to a national forest. The main house had just four bedrooms, but the guest house added another two.

Judy had stayed up past midnight searching all the Montana newspaper websites. She'd also purchased online subscriptions to *Big Sky Journal, Montana Living*, and *Montana* magazines. She'd also bought online subscriptions to several national magazines that target the rich, including *Robb Report, Private Air Luxury Homes, Swanky Retreats,* and *Architectural Digest.*

This morning she'd started searching them all. She decided on screens to limit the searches. For her to be interested, a person had to live in Montana and own at least 100 acres — or they had to visit the state at least four times a year. She also searched for men with powerful positions in the Montana or national government. Because of Rasmussen's position on the Energy Review Board, she gave extra weight to anyone associated with oil, coal, or alternative energy.

She went down a research rabbit hole with the big landowners. They were mostly individuals such as Ted Turner and Stan Kroenke and a few families. There was one surprise — the Church of Jesus Christ of Latter-day Saints owned 151,840 acres. There were three corporations in the top 15 — one focused on timber, another on "resource investment" (which was vague enough to mean anything), and one a Bahamian holding company. She'd texted those three names to Mason.

For today, she searched each online magazine and the newspapers for "Lodgepole Sanctuary," the name of the ranch. It took two hours and she only got ten hits. From them, she'd figure out who else in these circles might also have stayed there.

She emailed her spreadsheets to both Mason and Connor,

There was a knock at the door.

Judy looked out the peek hole and saw a brass badge covering almost all of the view. It said, "Sheriff" and "Flagstone County" with "State of Montana" in the center.

"I can see the badge," she told the door, "but I also need to see you."

The badge moved back, and she saw a pudgy man with porcine eyes and a brown-brimmed hat that looked like one worn by a Smoky-the-Bear-ad forrest ranger.

"What do you want?"

"Ma'am, we got a call from the homeowner of this house. They asked us to do a security check because a silent alarm was set off. I need to come in and make sure everything's alright."

"Why, that's most considerate of you, officer, but I'm just fine."

"I'm sorry, ma'am, but the concern was whether the *house* was fine. I need to step inside and do a quick look around. It won't take but a few minutes."

Judy wondered about him. "Please give me your name so I can call the sheriff's office to make sure you're who you say you are."

"Dwane Peabody, ma'am. Go right ahead."

The Sheriff's office confirmed the man really was one of their investigators, but Judy was still uneasy. She got her .22 and placed it under a towel on the kitchen counter. Open and concealed carry were both allowed here.

She patted her wristbands where she wore her modern-day hat pins, and she tapped her necklace to make sure it was still there.

Then she opened the door.

He nodded at her and looked at a notebook. "You're Jane Simpson?" he asked. It was the name on her fake I.D. that she'd used for the rental.

"Yes sir."

He smiled. "Pleased to meet you, ma'am," he said, holding out his right hand with a class ring on it.

She extended hers, and he shook it.

"Ow!" It felt like a bee sting in her palm. She jerked her hand away and looked at it.

"Wha...?" Judy turned and ran toward the kitchen counter and her gun. Or, rather, she tried.

It was so far away.

Belatedly, she remembered to push the hidden button sewn into her bra.

Then her vision went blurry, her knees buckled, and the floor rushed up to hit her.

## 23

## WOLF-SARA

I t was a great dream, so I was sorry to wake up.

I'd been lying on soft grass near a stream, with eyes-barely-opened pups climbing all over me, whining, nibbling my ears and play-attacking each other.

Danger? Is that why I woke?

I opened my eyes, but I couldn't see anything. I was covered in something.

Trapped?

No! I could move.

I stayed perfectly still and inhaled through my nose. I smelled blood! But no predators. I smelled prey animals — rabbits and squirrels. And, below me, bugs. Earth.

I turned my ears in every direction. Listening.

Normal, if muted, sounds of the night came to me. The rustle of feathers. Claws digging into dirt. The death of a bug in a bird's beak.

Then... a wolf howled. Another joined in. Soon more wolves howled than I had claws to count. They were singing their pack song. Their belonging to each other. Their vast numbers that warned anyone away from their land.

They were far away — too far for smell. So they didn't know I was here.

I was safe.

An annoying buzz came to my left ear. Again. It was the noises made by two-foot predators.

It said "Sah Rah" over and over.

Annoyed, I stood and shook a bunch of white, wet... snow!... off me. I looked around and up. More of the stuff was falling from the skies.

The noise blared again in my ear, so I shook my head hard. It didn't help!

I shook as hard as I could, and something fell from my ear.

No more noise! Very good.

Leave! There was danger here.

I smelled my own blood, but when I checked myself, I didn't feel hurt. I also smelled an older two-footer stink. A human. More danger.

I turned to where the wolves were still howling — something told me that was the way to go. For safety. But that pack was too large.

I turned my head slightly to the right of their location. That direction felt safe too — and I heard no wolves there.

Quietly, I started moving through the trees.

After a long while, the trees thinned out and I stopped, surveying the bare land in front of me.

There was a town ahead, but I saw no two-footers out. The snow was keeping them in their dens. Good.

I circled left to avoid the town, then raced across a highway.

Their smells faded as I continued on, distances melting away under my paws.

Far ahead I heard a single male wolf howl out the question — "Is anyone else out here alone and seeking?" His deep voice said he'd be big.

Interesting.

He wasn't part of the big pack to the left.

I would need a pack to survive. Large wolves are best when it comes to a fight.

Maybe...

And... he was in the direction I somehow needed to go.

I did not return his call.

But I turned and started towards the lone wolf.

# 24

## MASON

Mason was sure he was going to throw up.

He held a barf bag in his hands as the helicopter lifted from Bozeman. Looking outside didn't do a thing to ease his distress.

Losing contact with Sara had happened before.

He'd waited yesterday for her to enter the "007" code into her phone. After an hour went by, Mason started pacing. After two hours with no contact from her, Mason used the com into her ear.

He said her name softly. Then louder. Then he shouted.

Nothing.

He was supposed to have seen Mom's last girl last night, but he'd canceled. Instead, he'd caught the first plane to Bozeman, Montana, then the first helicopter to leave in the morning.

If only he'd been able to get a little sleep.

Outside the windows was a winter wonderland of snow-covered ground and white-decorated trees.

The trackers Mason had in Sara's microphone earrings and her button camera had not moved from where he last talked to her.

Right before the two gunshots.

Bile rose in his throat and spewed into the barf bag. The smell made him vomit again. The helicopter pilot looked back at him in disgust, probably making sure Mason was using a bag.

Finally, they landed at the coordinates he'd given Sara just the day before. Where the lithium test mine was drilled.

"I need to hike in a ways and then come back," he told the pilot.

He wore new snow hiking boots that were slightly too large and let his feet slip around inside. It was the only size he could get at the one stop he made. He zipped his also-new anorak up over his chin until just his eyes were exposed.

He looked at his GPS — he'd downloaded a cached map — and took off for the tracker coordinates.

Ten minutes later he'd found a small break in the trees, but there was no Sara.

He knew he was near.

He broadcast a monotone to the ear receiver she was wearing. But he heard nothing. He doubled the strength of the broadcast.

There. Near where the trees got denser. He tracked the sound.

He was having trouble breathing.

If she wasn't here — where was she? If she was here, was she... no. She could not be...

It took him several minutes to carefully dig down into 12 inches of snow, as well as the leaves and twigs under it.

There it was. Her earbud, his monotone coming from it, with no Sara anywhere in sight.

Feeling ghoulish, he tamped the snow down in a ten-foot radius of the earbud — and was relieved to find no body.

So, what happened?

She had to have been shot and it had to be bad — her heart or her head. If it had actually killed her, she'd be here. Wolf or human, she'd be here.

When she'd been shot in the lungs on the last mission, her body had transformed into a wolf automatically — to heal her. And it did.

She probably transformed this time, as well.

So where was she?

## 25

## JUDY

Judy awoke to hear two men arguing. She didn't recognize either voice.

She froze and took stock.

She was lying in a heap on a carpeted floor. She slitted her eyes open and found she was in the dark. She was facing a closed door with a small square window in it, about the size of her head.

The only light in the room came from the window.

She tried, but she couldn't understand what the men were saying, only that the tone and staccato of their words sounded hostile. Like serious cussing.

She took stock of herself. Her wristbands with her custom spikes were gone. She still had her necklace.

And… she still had her bra with the tracker hidden in it.

Slowly, she moved her hands until she could push the button. Again.

She'd have to give Connor a big sloppy kiss in thanks. The man was an amazing trainer.

He'd warned her that uncertain situations were the biggest danger because you tried to tell yourself nothing was wrong. He'd said to trust her 'lizard brain.' If it raised even the tiniest question about a person or a situation — she would already be in deep trouble.

"What's the first thing you do?" he had asked her over and over. The correct answer was "Raise the alarm." He told her she could always let them know later if the alarm was false. What she couldn't do was send the alarm if she was already unconscious.

The alarm didn't track her continuously — it only gave her location when it was pushed. But now that she'd pushed it again, hopefully...

There was a noise at her door.

Judy lay perfectly still, eyes closed.

The door opened. The air in the room, which had been still as a grave, suddenly swirled with life.

She heard a small, metallic noise, then the bang of the door closing.

She didn't move.

Judy heard more talking, and this time she could understand it.

"She saw my face. Why is she still alive?"

The words were muffled but clear, sending shards of icicles into her heart. They were just on the other side of the door, probably watching her in the small window.

"Nothing else happens until after Thursday. Nothing."

"So on Friday?"

The voice trailed off and she couldn't hear the response. They had left.

Judy slitted her eyes open again. The metallic noise had been a metal tray of food dropped on the floor just inside the door.

She opened her eyes fully, pretending she had just woken up.

She looked around but didn't see any cameras in the room.

But would she? She needed to talk to Mason and find out what they looked like — or if they were too small to see.

She wondered who would come to get her — Sara or Connor? And how far away they were.

Today was Sunday, unless she'd slept a lot longer than she thought. On Thursday something important was happening. After that, it would be just fine to kill her. And... maybe Dakota, too?

She had four and a half days left to live. But Sara or Connor would be here for her long before that. Hopefully, in just a few hours.

She had to believe it.

## 26

### WOLF-SARA

The snow stopped well before daylight, but I continued my trek.

This land smelled like happiness. There was no two-footer stink, no machine stink, no noises that hurt your ears. Just land as far as I could see or smell or hear.

And prey everywhere to fill the belly.

I heard warning howls from the big wolf pack to my left. I heard an answering howl from a wolf in the same direction but much farther away. Then, a chorus of wolves from that distance.

This place was crawling with wolf packs!

I turned farther right and continued running. In the distance I saw a lone, black-fur wolf standing in the open. He looked strong. He scented the air, but he couldn't smell me. The wind came to me, not to him, telling me he was young, two or three summers. Of course. Why else would he have left his pack?

I started loping towards him. Gradually I caught the scents of another male and a female. Three would be good. More would be a danger to me.

When I reached where I'd seen the wolf, he slipped quietly from behind a rock and stared at me.

I stopped, too. His fur was thick and shiny and my nose told me he was healthy. He was big — almost as big as me.

He moved to a solitary, scrawny tree and peed, marking his territory.

I smelled a patch near me where the female had marked, and I peed over hers.

A high-pitched bark came from the trees and out rushed the female — barking and nipping at the big male and at the second male who came out to join her.

She urged them to challenge me, and they considered it.

The female was smart. She knew she needed the two males to drive me away. They would do that — join with her — if she convinced them I was a danger to the pack.

However... if this was just a dominance contest between two females? She'd be on her own.

I turned my back and walked four steps away, then I turned and sat my rump down on the ground.

The big male looked at me, then sat his butt on the ground as well. The smaller male copied him.

The female launched herself at me, flying through the air — jaws open — to grab my throat. I zigged my head away from her jaws, then turned back as she flew past me, grabbed her shoulders in my jaws and threw her to the ground.

Then I released her and stepped away, again sitting down, showing I was no threat.

She regrouped and came for me again. I had to admire her spunk, given how much bigger I was. This time I pinned her with my jaws around her neck and a paw on her chest — holding her down.

Still, she struggled.

I didn't want to hurt her — I liked her spirit — but I was not going to sleep without this settled. I squeezed my jaws just a bit more — drawing blood.

Was she really going to make me...?

She stopped struggling. She even peed a little.

I accepted her submission and released her.

We spent the rest of the day lazing on the hills and napping in the sun. The big one came over and lay near me. I liked his company.

By the time the sun sank, we were all restless. We got up and started moving, away from the big packs. We loped through the night, silent as smoke. Where patches of trees had shielded from the sun, we saw hoof prints in the snow from large prey. They smelled delicious.

There was a flurry of movement and the female trotted up to me, a white-colored rabbit in her jaws. My mouth watered, but my head-voice screamed, *no!*, so I left it to her.

We traveled through the night until, in the morning, we hit a wall of wolf smell. Wolves had claimed the territory ahead of us. I smelled the pee of at least nine of them.

We were just four, so we heeded the warning. Better to stay here than to go onto their land.

I looked around and liked what I saw. We could live well here. It could be home.

Now I just needed to figure out why my head-voice didn't want me to eat. How long could I comply?

Not eat? It made no sense.

# 27

## CONNOR

Connor stared through a scope at what he could see of the house nestled in the trees about a quarter mile away. The building looked huge — at least 5,000 square feet. That's not even counting the two outbuildings he couldn't see that Google Earth said were there.

The land he'd hiked through was densely forested, but he didn't know how much of it was owned by this place.

He'd almost had a heart attack when Judy's panic button pinged him. The location was her Big Sky townhome, but she was gone when he got there.

Mason called to say he'd got Judy's ping, too. Sara would have also.

"Sara can't come," Mason had told Connor. "It's up to you."

Connor had stayed at the townhouse, pacing, waiting for another ping so he'd know which direction she'd gone. After an hour of nothing, then another, he knew she had to be unconscious. Or worse.

He called a pet hotel, gave them his credit card number, and they came and took Judy's cat.

This morning, her tracker finally pinged again. It was 47 miles away, just north of West Yellowstone and almost on the border with Yellowstone Park.

He'd called Mason when he got the second ping, but the kid uncharacteristically blew him off, sounding rushed and eager to get off the phone. "Call me for something specific you need, but otherwise I've got no time."

When Connor decided to join this crazy band of do-gooders, he realized he'd often be working alone. He'd provisioned himself for a bunch of different situations.

However, a huge house full of an unknown number of hostiles and innocents was more than he was willing to tackle blindly. If he couldn't have Sara — and he wondered what she was doing that was more important than rescuing Judy — he at least needed intel.

He'd marked down the license number of a truck that arrived pulling a trailer with "Joe's Snow & Grow" on the side. Last night dropped a dusting of snow over the mounds left from the blizzard two days ago.

Two guys jumped out and worked two different snowblowers to clear the sidewalks around the houses and on the driveways. With another blizzard expected tonight, the men must have all the snow-removal work they could want.

He considered going after them when they left, but odds were they never went into the houses.

It was 3:30 in the afternoon, with about an hour left of daylight, when he saw a beat-up old Kia Rio drive out from where the servant's entrance had to be. The scope showed a woman with gray hair and tired eyes driving.

He got the license plate, then returned to his rental SUV.

He lost her on the short drive to West Yellowstone when he got stuck behind a semi. He called Mason for the woman's address.

Mason answered with an aggressive, "What now?"

"What now?" Connor asked. "Are you too busy on one of those dates your mom set up to give a shit about helping me rescue Judy?"

There was silence on the phone, then Connor heard Mason take a big breath.

"Sorry," Mason said. "Sorry. I'm dealing with some complicated... What do you need?"

"An address for this license plate in West Yellowstone." Connor read off the numbers.

Connor waited, then wrote down the address Mason gave him.

"Hey," he said. "You alright?"

"I'm fine," Mason said, hanging up.

Like hell he was.

And where was Sara? He could use her for this op. He'd never had a woman on his teams in Special Forces, but Sara had managed to get through four armed men to rescue him in Arizona.

And, yes, that still stung — her rescuing him.

He also wished he'd seen her in action instead of just seeing the surprisingly bloody dead-body aftermath. He wondered why she hadn't just shot them.

Regardless... he could use another fighter to go get Judy.

Except Sara was "out of state and undercover." It was unusually mysterious... and damned inconvenient.

The location Mason gave him was an apartment in one of three look-alike, brick-box buildings, with dirt, not lawn, showing through some shoveled patches in the snow. A lonely kid's bike was locked to one of the entrance railings.

Connor found Eliana Contreras' apartment number and knocked on the door.

The woman who answered was the woman he'd seen leaving the house. She looked out from the slit opening, her door's chain lock on.

This would be tricky. Connor had trouble with the "getting people to trust and help you" aspect of the job. Not company execs. He knew how to bond with them.

Women were the problem — his size made them wary.

"Ma'am," he said, "I need your help to save a woman's life." He passed her one of the business cards Judy had made for him.

"She and I are both investigators with Last Chance Investigations down in Tulsa. We're up here looking for a missing woman..." he pulled out his phone and showed her Dakota's picture. "Have you seen her?"

The woman looked carefully, then said, "No."

Connor nodded, thoughtfully, then slid his thumb to show Judy's picture.

"Have you seen my partner?"

The woman looked up at him, her brows furrowed in surprise.

"That's right, my partner has now gone missing as well. I'm pretty sure I know where she is — right at that house you just left this morning. At least, I know her cell phone was there. Did you see her this morning?"

The woman shook her head. "No."

"She would not be there of her own free will. Her cell phone is in the farthest out guesthouse. May I show you?"

The woman stared at him, then at his card. "One minute." She shut the door in his face, and he could hear her lock it.

As a minute passed, then more, he hoped she was calling the number on his card instead of the police. And he hoped Mason was sounding professional instead of how he last responded to Connor.

Finally, she opened the door again. "Come in," she said, backing away to give him room.

The small living area led right into a tiny kitchen with a small island that served as both a counter and a dining table. She sat in one of the kitchen chairs and offered him the other.

"Show me," she said.

He showed her the buildings from Google Earth and pointed to the one where Judy's phone had been.

She looked up. "I clean the main house and this other house..." she pointed to the cottage closest to the main house."

She pointed to the house where Judy's tracker was, "I never clean this house."

Connor thought. "Okay, let me ask you about the number of people in the main house and that first guest house."

An hour later, Connor was back near the compound where he hoped Judy still was. He parked on a back road, as close as he dared. He didn't know if he'd have to carry her to get her away.

When he first came to Montana for this case, he'd bought a white & tan ski suit loose enough to go over his clothes, including his

Kevlar vest. It wouldn't be as good as snow camo for approaching the house, but it was close.

More important — it didn't scream military.

Connor had also considered the problem of going after someone in the midst of a bunch of civilians. He needed a way to stop the civilians from interfering without shooting bullets into them.

His solution? He bought two taser guns that each shot three cartridges. The guns were bulkier than normal tasers, but it would be worth it in exactly the mess of a situation he was looking at right now. He added six extra cartridges in his outside pockets.

He would approach the guest house on the side facing away from the other two houses. His entire strategy consisted of get in, get Judy and get out. Incapacitate anyone who tried to stop him.

He grinned to himself. Just like some of the missions in Afghanistan.

*See,* he told himself, *I'm not getting too old for this shit. Forty is the new twenty, right?*

Except... it wasn't as much fun alone.

Speaking of which... he put in his earbuds and called Mason. "I'm about ready to go in," he said. "What can you tell me?"

"You must be in the right place," Mason said, "because I still haven't been able to get into their phone system — it has serious highest-level encryption — stuff it would take me a day to break into. I can see the bandwidth being used, but I can't get the content. About all I'll be able to tell you is if there's a sudden spike in traffic."

"So you can tell me if they've spotted me."

"Probably."

"Probably?"

"If your appearance is a surprise — so they have to alert people — I'll see the increased traffic. If they're just laying in wait for you with pre-assigned responses, then no. I won't have a clue."

"Great."

Connor slipped thermal goggles over his ski cap and tilted the lenses up. He didn't need them to see — once the sun set, there would be a half moon and more stars than he'd seen anywhere except Afghanistan.

But he would want to know if there were men in the woods. Or bears.

The forest of pines surrounding the house was dense, so he moved slowly, making sure of his footing.

He doubted they had tripwire sensors in the trees — they'd be getting non-stop false alarms from wildlife. But they might very well have cameras set up for the treeless land that surrounded the house.

He'd be exposed for those last 30 yards.

He paused at the edge where the trees stopped and studied the target close-up. There were six heat signatures inside the guest house — six he could see. There could be more. He assumed two more men were patrolling the grounds, although he'd seen no sign of them.

He didn't have direct line-of-sight to the next guest house. Eliana Contreras thought there were four men staying in that house, but there could be more. Many more.

If there were cameras ahead, men from the next house could get within shooting distance in about three minutes. Four or five minutes if he could keep the house between him and where they'd be coming from.

Two of the heat signatures were isolated. The other four were together. He hoped Judy was one of the isolated signatures.

If not... well... he had a 17-round magazine in his silenced Glock 19 and two more in his pockets.

# 28

## CONNOR

The one-story guest house Connor prepared to attack looked like a rich person's idea of a cabin, not a real one. Big enough for three or four bedrooms. It had lots of glass on the front of it, and on the back were full-wall glass sliders leading out to a large deck. Inside, he expected a wide-open designer space where everyone could see everyone — the only private areas being the bedrooms and baths.

He was facing a side of the house where all that extra glass disappeared. There were only two windows here, neither of them big. Both were covered with closed wood shutters. They were undoubtedly bedrooms, but were not meant for rich guests — not with those tiny windows.

If he was lucky, one of the two heat signatures in those rooms was Judy. Get in, grab her, get out. Avoid the four heat signatures hanging out in the main area.

Unlikely, however.

As von Moltke learned, when fighting on two fronts at the start of World War I — no battle plan survives first contact with the enemy.

He waited until the last glimpses of daylight surrendered to the dark.

Connor found it interesting that no lights shown from the two target windows. Either nobody was in them or those shutters were designed to block all the light.

Enough thinking.

He tapped his com. "You with me?" he asked Mason, wanting to be sure. The kid had been a little squirrelly the past two days.

A voice in his ear said, "I'm here."

Connor patted all his pocketed extra weapons with his PIG alpha gloves and said, "Showtime."

He slipped from the trees, using only the starlight to guide his steps and to alert him to any patches of ice.

He walked confidently towards the house — as fast as he could move while pretending to be a guard making the rounds. That might give him an extra second before someone shot at him.

The only sound was the swish of his boots going in and out of the snow-covered ground.

He saw nobody.

He walked straight up to the side of the house between the two windows and pressed his back against the wall. "Anything?" he asked softly.

"No increased traffic yet."

The two heat signatures on this side of the house were separated, one in the front room and one in the back. Connor took a quick glance at the shutters on the back window.

Then he looked again.

He touched them and found no give at all.

They looked like closed window shutters, but they weren't. Instead, they were a single block of solid wood designed to look like two shutters. It was tightly secured to the house.

He moved past them and glanced around the corner to the back of the house. Seeing nobody, he moved to the small back window for that corner room. It also had pretend shutters that were a solid block of wood.

He wasn't getting into this room or the one on the front without going inside the house.

He heard a noise behind him and dropped to a squat, bringing up his gun hand.

Nobody.

He waited a couple of seconds, and then a white-cammo-clad man poked his head around the corner. The man had planned to look and jerk back.

Connor recognized the body twitch as the man stopped his backward motion and tried to lower his MP5 SD down to where Connor was instead of where the weapon was originally pointed.

Connor shot him in the forehead and he fell back, his MP5 rising up toward the sky and firing twice before his fingers stopped obeying his commands.

Connor didn't worry about the noise from the machine gun — with its integral suppressor, it wouldn't be more than 70 decibels.

The suppressor on Connor's pistol still allowed 134 decibels. If they didn't hear that, they weren't listening.

And they had to be listening.

"Screw it," he said, grabbing the automatic from the dead man. He took a fresh magazine as well, then moved to the back patio.

He tried the glass sliding doors, but they were locked. He aimed the MP5 and blew out the glass, then kicked the shards and entered.

Two men, who'd been watching a huge HDTV, rose from the sofa and pointed their identical MP5s at him. He used the last of the magazine to permanently stop them.

Quickly, he slammed in the second magazine.

In his ear, Mason said, "Phone traffic jumped. Next house and the main house. Company coming."

Connor dropped to the floor and picked up a second fallen MP5. He pointed it down a hall and killed a man there who had, stupidly, brought a pistol to a machine-gun fight.

Where was the fourth man? Connor looked and saw the front door open. A ruse?

No time.

He tore down the hall and kicked in the back bedroom door.

Judy, thank god! Standing. Looking pissed.

A man was behind her, holding a pistol at her head. Finger on the trigger.

Connor didn't register the threats coming from the man's mouth.

He saw Judy's left hand at her neck, tight on the necklace, its razor edge extending up an inch and a half. She'd already released the chain, which was hanging down on each side.

Connor raised his MP5 to the roof.

He said, "Sure, man, whatever you want. Just don't hurt her."

He saw the man relax just a tad, the pistol barrel pulling about an inch away from her head.

"Stupid," the man said to him, moving the barrel of his gun towards Connor.

Connor saw Judy's body turn slightly. She grabbed her left hand, holding the necklace, with her right and used both to slice down hard on the man's inside wrist.

The pressure forced his hand away, and his shot missed Connor.

The rush of blood told him Judy had severed the man's radial artery, but Connor wasn't interested in waiting 30 seconds for him to pass out.

He moved his MP5 back and shot the man in the head.

"Let's go," Connor said, turning away.

"Not yet," Judy said running to the next bedroom door. "I think they're holding someone here too."

"But..." He stopped his objection.

"Step back," he said, before kicking in this door as well. A girl lay on the bed, but Connor first cleared the room.

"It's Dakota!" Judy said.

"We have to go — now!"

The girl just sat there, eyes wide.

Judy put her hands on the girl's shoulders and pulled her forward, saying, "C'mon, sweetie, we're being rescued by this handsome man. Let's get out of here!"

Connor winced when he saw the girl. He knew she was 18, but she looked three years younger than that. Long, black hair pulled back, no makeup, all she needed was a high-school uniform.

The red in her eyes and the bruised look of her skin under them spoke of no sleep and crying.

She grabbed Judy and hugged her hard.

"Now!" Connor said.

*More hostiles possible in two minutes,* Connor reminded himself.

He hurried them back to the great room, then — after checking for newly-arrived enemies who weren't here yet — out the broken glass door.

"Judy," he said, handing her his cell phone and pointing towards the end of the house and beyond. "You run as fast as you can to the trees right there. Then keep going. The car's about a quarter mile in that direction, key under the driver's floor mat."

Her brows knit together. "You?"

"I'll be right behind you."

Judy grabbed Dakota's hand and said, "Girl, run like your life depends on it."

Connor ran right on their tail, searching the woods ahead and to both sides. Then, after a minute and a half, he added frequent backward checks.

Another minute went by with the only sounds he heard being the swish of the snow, the stomp of their footsteps and gasps for breath.

They'd made it into the trees and were halfway to the car when a torrent of suppressed bullets fired behind them.

Then it stopped.

*Idiots,* thought Connor, trotting behind the women, trying to mentally prod them to run faster. *You multiply fifty decibels by four or five guns, and you're making enough noise for someone to call the cops.*

They kept running. Soon they could see the SUV — about 200 yards away.

Connor saw a muzzle flash from his side. Not from behind.

He fell down, feeling like Godzilla had punched him. Good thing he had IIIA+ side panels in his vest.

He saw Judy reach the car and pull Dakota into the back seat. She slammed that door, then opened the driver's door. She looked back for Connor.

Horror crossed her face and she lurched to run to him.

"Save Dakota," he yelled at her. "Go now."

She got that stubborn-mule look on her face that Connor recognized.

Then the man who'd shot him turned his MP5 on her and she

dove back into the car. Bullets peppered it as she started it, lurched it into drive and took off.

Connor's ribs hurt like a sonofagun. They would have hurt much worse with cheaper plates in his vest.

While the shooter spent another second trying to stop the fleeing vehicle, Connor pulled his Glock 19 from his pocket and fired two shots into the man's head.

Connor forced his feet under him and stood.

"Mase," he said into his mike. "Judy's on my phone and she's got Dakota. Tell her to drive north towards Bozeman. Now. I'll wait."

After a minute, Mason said in his ear, "Done. What about you?"

"Don't let her actually get to Bozeman. That's a rental car. They could track it. There's really only three ways she could go from here, so they could stake out all three. Can you get a helicopter to her before the new blast of snow starts? Somewhere along the road?"

"I'll check. Now what about you?"

"Only two ways I could go — east into the foothills or west into the Park."

Connor saw movement in the trees to his left.

And more movement. Three men at least.

"Into the Park it is," he said as he took off running.

"Weapons?" asked Mason.

"Fourteen shots left in my Glock, plus 34 in the extra magazines. Plus whatever's left in this automatic. And I have my knives. Don't worry. I could take over a small country with what I've got."

"But..."

"I've seen the topo maps of this area. Lots of small canyons where I could stage a trap."

"But..."

"Get Judy and Dakota first. If there's still time before the blizzard, come get me next. But I'm good for overnight if I need to."

"You're sure?"

"Do it! I'm wasting air talking to you now."

Mason's voice went away.

Highway 191 came up pretty quickly. Connor waited for the only car in sight to disappear before he rushed across it. A large, running river was to his right. Fortunately, it turned southeast while he ran directly east. He could not risk getting wet.

Why wasn't it frozen?

He shook his head. Irrelevant.

He continued on. Fifteen minutes later, he hit a copse of trees and stopped to tie his boots tighter. He was running too slow — trying to prevent a turned ankle on the uneven, sometimes-snow-packed, sometimes-icy ground.

The night wasn't a problem — the stars and the reflections off the snow gave his eyes plenty of light to see.

Thirty-five minutes, he told himself. That would get him five miles in — probably to that forested area he could see ahead.

He grinned. Well... maybe a tiny bit more than 35 minutes. He was in his late 40s now, after all.

He took off at a faster pace.

As he ran, he conducted a mental SITREP. Positives: he had plenty of ammo, neutral terrain, night-vision goggles, warm clothes, and poorly-trained men behind him. And an active link to Mason.

Negatives? Blizzard starting soon. Would his chasers have thermal scopes? If so... he wondered how many bears or bison were in this section of the Park. Not bison, he decided. They'd be in a herd — so they'd offer no confusion with his heat signature.

Bears would be good.

None of those idiots chasing him would have had thermal scopes on them, but they could have gone back for them.

Although... the guy on patrol who shot his vest might have had them. He was dead, but Connor assumed they had two out.

The other could be coming after him.

The main question was: Did they only have tough-guy idiot shooters or did they also have men who knew what they were doing?

Who knew how to track a man?

He had to assume they'd send someone like that after him with a bunch of backup.

He smiled and kept running.

# 29

## CONNOR

From topo maps, Connor knew most of the land here was far too open for his purposes.

When he entered Yellowstone, he was able to see for miles even though it was night. The snow and the thin air bounced around the light from a gazillion visible stars, making the ground as clear as if it were just dusk.

At night it also looked like an alien landscape.

He passed a "forest" of bare trees 8-12 feet tall and skinny as straight pins. They looked like sharpened punji sticks from some giant's tiger pit.

He smiled again. Appropriate thoughts for a man being hunted.

The snow coated acres of heather plants, which released a sweet floral smell as he stomped his way across them.

Finally, he reached the trees he'd first seen in the distance.

He passed them by for something better another mile ahead — dense pines, firs and spruce trees, plus bush cover in a line as far as his eyes could see. They marked the location of a riverbed or stream and lower land where he could hide.

The snow started then, light at first but quickly turning into rivers of snow. Visibility shrank to ten feet. Then to two feet. It would cover all his tracks. But it wouldn't help much if his chasers had thermal scopes.

"Mason," he said into his mike.

He heard only static.

"Mase?"

"Ghzzzzzzht... Judy and... bzzzztt... safe, pzzzaat... you tomorrow...."

"Repeat, the women are safe and I'm here for the night? Correct?"

"Bzzzztt...."

"I'm turning off the system on my end, so don't panic. We'll talk tomorrow."

He shut it down but left the earpiece and mike in place for tomorrow.

For now, Connor needed to build a snow cave. Both to keep him warm and to block thermal imaging.

He scooped snow up in his gloves to compact it into ice, only to find he couldn't. The snow didn't melt into a solid from squishing it together. It slipped out of his gloves in separate grains, like rice.

Dry snow! Supposedly great for skiing on, but not for what he wanted.

*Okay*, he thought. *Plan B.*

He found a promising spot where the ground dropped down about six feet, so he'd have a wall of earth between him and any approaching hunter. Using his knife, he cut off small branches of fir — eight to ten feet in length and laid them against the top of the drop-off, putting the stronger, wider ends on the ground about three feet out from the bank. He stacked them thick so the snow would pile on top instead of falling through. Then he took smaller fir branches and laid them as a flooring to keep him off the snow floor.

He moved inside the shelter and used an extra-dense branch to close his "door." This would work.

He stretched and evaluated his bruised ribs. Painful. But he'd managed with much worse.

He pulled out one knife and lay it next to his hand, right next to the MP5 SD that still had a few rounds in it and which was much quieter than his silenced Glock. To the pile, he added one of his tasers as a last-chance-hail-Mary in case everything went FUBAR - Fucked Up Beyond All Recognition.

He heard no animal sounds. No birds. The only noise was the whoosh of the wind as it ran free over the open spaces — only to slam hard against the tops of the trees near him.

Would they come for him in this weather? Not if all they had was meat-head shooters. They'd get turned around in all this and probably end up shooting each other. Which would turn a PR mess they could hide into a huge, visible problem.

Somebody good? A tracker? Only if he was already at the houses or could be there within 10-15 minutes of when Connor left. And only if he had a thermal scope.

No... Connor corrected himself. Such a man could have left an hour after Connor if he was on a snowmobile. But the noise would give him away.

Unless... hadn't he read?... somebody was making electric snowmobiles. It wasn't something he'd paid much attention to, living in Oklahoma and working for CEOs in major cities.

He thought he'd read they had a limited range... although that wasn't a problem here. At most he was ten miles into the Park... probably less.

The article said they had a completely silent engine, but they still made noise when they moved — from the treads tearing into and tossing up the snowpack they rode on.

Connor was a firm believer in planning for the absolute worst that could happen. As a soldier, you could depend on it. As a bodyguard, it happened sometimes.

Here? The odds were against someone coming without making enough noise to alert him. And, even if they did, his thermal signature should be gone or almost gone for anyone coming from the west.

But it was possible.

He needed to listen like his life depended on it — but all he could hear was the constant howl of the wind.

It was irritating, like a fingernail on a blackboard.

His hands were cold.

His hat, snow suit and boots were all good. Not to mention his body armor. But he'd gone for lighter shooting gloves instead of stay-overnight-in-a-snow-cave mittens. He alternated putting one of them after the other under an armpit. He needed one hand close to his gun at all times. Just in case.

His eyes opened.

He must have dozed off and let his head drop back against the embankment. He picked up the MP5 and held it halfway between shooting straight ahead and shooting up towards the top of the drop-off.

What woke him?

He listened, hard. The wind was screaming louder than before. Was there another noise? Something like churning snow?

He strained, but he couldn't distinguish a separate noise from the wind.

He hated sitting there, making himself an easier target. But he would freeze to death outside of this snow cave. And leaving would knock off a lot of the snow cover that kept him warm and hid him both visually and thermally.

However, a smart someone could figure it out.

Connor lay down on his left side on the branches, making himself a harder target. The MP5 was in his right hand, the stock of it braced against his left shoulder. His Glock was in his left hand, his main knife out and lying next to him. His backup knife was in a waist sheathe. His backup gun was in an ankle holster.

On edge, he waited. And waited. And waited.

He awoke to a spray of bullets, stitching through his snow cave from his head to his feet.

If he'd been sitting up...

He tightened his hands on his MP5 and sent a spray of bullets out, finishing up the magazine.

Grabbing his Glock and his knife, he lunged up and out, pushing the snow-laden branches of his cave out — overbalancing himself to do it — hoping to hit his attacker. He needed to see what he was facing.

The man was down, about 15 feet from Connor, so Connor

continued his overbalance, falling forward and rolling quickly to the man.

He ended up closer than he'd planned, his Glock out.

He wondered what kind of intel he could get from the man.

*Get your head straight!*

Like a snake striking, the man moved fast, knife in hand, aiming for the artery in Connor's groin.

Connor twisted, but the knife plunged to the hilt into his right leg. Connor felt something snap and his leg buckled, no longer under his control.

Connor placed his silenced Glock against the side of the man's head and pulled the trigger. The man collapsed.

There was blood everywhere.

How much of it was his?

Connor looked quickly at his thigh. It was bleeding way too fast, but it was seeping out, not spurting. The man had missed his artery.

Then the pain hit.

His leg was on fire!

He rolled, over and a whole new level of pain nearly blacked him out.

*Shii-it!*

Carefully, he tested the leg. He could move it backward a little, but it wouldn't go forward. Impossible. Not because of the pain. He could get past that.

Maybe.

But the leg simply wouldn't extend forward. He must have a severed tendon.

Blood first. Connor opened the snowsuit of the dead man. Between the blood and the bullet, he wasn't getting facial recognition from this guy. Ever. Connor used his knife to cut the man's sweater and shirt off, the shirt into strips.

He wrapped his leg tight to stop the blood loss. He didn't let himself scream when he tightened the strips, but he sure as hell wanted to.

Connor looked around. He saw nobody else. He wondered how

far the guy's snowmobile was. Could he? No... wherever it was, it was too far away.

The blood-bath circle that surrounded him was disappearing. The snow was coming down so heavy that it would all be covered in a few minutes.

He had to get back to his cave or freeze to death.

But his shelter was no more.

He looked at the spray of fir branches spread out all around him and knew he wasn't re-building what he had.

He reached out and grabbed all the branches close to him.

There was a stone nearby, rising a little over two feet above the snow. He started to dig down into the snow beside it, feeling again how cold his hands were.

He looked at the body. The man had better gloves than Connor, so Connor stripped them off, put them on, and finished digging.

He moved by dragging his sitting butt around with his arms — it was all he could do. Even so, he couldn't stop the occasional jolt of pain strong enough that his vision whited out.

The stone was four feet tall when Connor had dug all the way down to the dirt it rested on. He placed fir branches down on the ground. Then he placed the remaining branches he'd gathered on top of the stone, angling down into another — smaller — lean-to formation. He pulled the man's body close by. Once it froze, it would work like a tree branch to protect him from the snow.

Before that... Connor stripped him of the snowsuit — cutting it off to preserve the maximum square footage of fabric.

Connor spread the material on the floor of his new cave-to-be.

He took all the man's weapons, including an MP5 SD — they must have bought them by the dozen — and a very nice Bowie eight-inch combat knife of stainless steel with a black passivate blade coating.

The man carried no driver's license or identification. He had $500 in his pocket which Connor added to the stash on his tiny new "floor."

He gave a big sigh of relief when he found a liter bottle of water on the man. Yes, he was surrounded by snow, but it was worthless without something to melt it so it wouldn't lower his body temperature.

Finally, having done all he could to ensure his survival overnight, he crawled into his tiny little cell and covered his opening with the remaining branches.

He relaxed the tense muscles in his neck and back. He sipped the water.

Then he heard sounds that made the hairs on the back of his neck stand up.

Wolf howls.

One. Then two. Then another.

*Oh. My. God.*

The snow might cover the blood, but it wouldn't cover the smell. And he had a nice, big, fat piece of meat lying right beside his hidey-hole.

He did not, not, not(!) want to move his leg. But neither did he want to be eaten by wolves.

He forced himself to haul his butt out of the shelter. He grabbed the man's body and laid him on the ground, perpendicular to the slope of the ground. Then, he pushed as hard as he could.

The body rolled maybe five feet and stopped.

No, no, no!

Large snowflakes dropped from the sky into his eyes. He shook his head, then he dragged his butt down to the man, and pushed again, rolling the body another five feet.

He looked back up to his tiny shelter and knew that was his limit. The 10 feet had to be far enough away because that was all he could do.

He was weak. He recognized it as coming from his blood loss. And from the pain of moving.

Slowly, painfully, he used his arms to drag his butt up the ten feet to his shelter and to crawl back inside.

He took another drink of water, then placed the bottle inside his jacket to keep the water warm.

He turned on his com system.

"Mase? You there?"

The static was still there. He heard, "... Connor? ... okay?"

"Not okay," he replied. He opened the wallet of the man he'd killed. "Man came after me. He's no longer a threat but he damaged my leg badly enough that I'm not walking out of here. Tonight is okay, but I'll need exfil tomorrow. Did you copy?"

"... snow let up... noon... you okay... then?"

"Maybe. Mase, I hear wolves. And there's a dead body 10 feet from my shelter."

Mason's voice came over at twice the volume, "...*not* kill a wolf... or jail... promise me!"

"If they try to kill me...."

"Wolves... afraid of humans... promise me... Under *no* circumstances...."

"See you tomorrow," Connor said and turned off the com to save the battery.

Yes, he could picture the fallout if he killed a Yellowstone wolf in the Park. And Mason was right — he'd never heard of a wolf attacking a human unless provoked.

But if one of them tried to get in his shelter... all bets were off.

# 30

## WOLF-SARA

I was curled up next to my pack, my tail covering my nose, keeping all my warm breaths heating up my body instead of disappearing into the air. I could feel each of my three pack mates, their bodies snug against mine. I closed my eyes, falling back into sleep.

Something startled me awake — an annoying noise, a buzzing like a very large bee.

I looked up and saw a black bug hovering in the air above us. As I stared at it, the thing came closer. Then it started to talk. Two-legger talk.

"Sah Rah," it said. "Sah rah Lor Ess."

It was beyond annoying.

I put my paws over my ears and buried my head further down into the snow. But it didn't help.

I got up, shaking the white stuff from my fur. I walked away from my pack and peed. The thing followed me.

"Sah Rah Lor Ess," it kept saying, over and over.

The noise hurt my head, so I shook it and shook it. But it wouldn't go away. I looked up and wished I could jump that high and kill it.

The voice changed. Now it was saying, "Cah nahs een tra blah," Again and again.

I stalked back to my pack mates, who were covered in snow except for three heads raised in curiosity at me. The black bug moved down, closer to me. Then I saw a fire spark, heard a funny squawk, and the machine dropped to the ground. Now silent.

Cautiously, I went to it. When it didn't move, I nosed it. It was dead. To make sure it stayed dead, I bit it in half and shook my head — sending pieces of it flying in all directions.

I lay down again next to my pack and tried to go back to sleep. But I couldn't.

There was something familiar about the bug. And the two-legger talk.

Finally I gave up. I was restless. I trotted back to some of the pieces. Even though the snow had covered it, I still knew where it was. It smelled like fire and two-legger machines.

Somehow, even dead, it kept annoying me.

My head jolted up. Did I hear another one? Yes!

There it was! Something blue was hanging down from its jaws.

I stared as the bug came nearer. When it got close enough, I leapt up and snatched at the hanging blue thing. When I did, the bug let go of it.

It dropped right on me. It had a smell... a familiar smell... a two-legged smell.

The black bug started talking again. The same words, "Cah nahs een tra blah,"

The noises went with the smell somehow. I buried my nose in the cloth and was surrounded by a very familiar smell. Connor's smell.

Connor?

"Connor's in trouble!" That was the words. "Connor's in trouble."

Connor Rockwood?

His smells. His name. And suddenly I saw the man, his shit-eating grin as he killed a man who was about to kill me.

Me. Sara Flores.

I sat back on my haunches, stunned.

I jumped up and used my jaws to pick up the blue thing the machine — the drone — had dropped. The thing with Connor's smell.

It was his underwear!

I dropped it like a rock.

Eww! Yuck!

Wait. "Connor's in trouble?"

I looked up at the drone. It had to be Mason.

"Sara Flores?" it said.

I nodded. Then I put my right front paw behind my ear — to show him I understood.

"Connor can't move," Mason's voice said through the drone, "and we can't get to him in this storm. He's about 5 miles south of you. The problem is — he hears wolves. Lots of wolves."

I nodded. There were at least nine wolves in the pack south of me.

"They'll come for him. There's a dead body — meat — just outside his shelter. Can you get there? Protect him until the snow stops and I can pick him up?"

I nodded my snout, but I wasn't sure. Protect him against nine wolves?

I had to leave. I looked around and my three pack mates were staring at me. Oh no...

Could I abandon them? Would they be able to survive — tucked in between three bigger packs?

I looked at the big male and felt a pang of regret.

Then flat-out horror.

OMG! I was... I would have... Thank god I didn't...

There probably isn't enough alcohol in the world to be able to wipe that from my mind if I had...

I just couldn't think about it.

I snarled at those who used to be my pack. I threatened them to make them stay where they were. Then, I turned and followed the lead of the drone. South. Through the snow.

The female came after me. I nipped at her, snarled and chased her away. Once I turned back. The big male was standing there where I'd left him. He watched me leave.

I felt like a total cad. I'd promised them my strength. My loyalty. Instead, I was abandoning them.

Mason told me he was leading me in a straight line to Connor. That I couldn't get lost because I'd find the blood smells. It was good to know because 10 minutes later the drone sparked and dropped dead. I just kept running.

A half-hour later, I smelled the blood.

# 31

## WOLF-SARA

I was deep in another pack's territory. I could smell the pack's mother and father and their young. They smelled healthy. Strong. These were not wolves I wanted to make my enemies. And... they smelled like... huh.

Maybe...?

But I couldn't think about that now.

I reached the bloodbath and assessed the situation. Connor smells came from a clump of snow, which probably hid a very tiny lean-to.

Not 10 feet from him I could smell a dead man, covered completely in snow. Grateful the pack wasn't here yet, I dug into the snow, found the guy and clamped my teeth down hard on his almost-frozen shoulder.

The meat made my mouth water. It had been three days with no food. I carefully did *not* swallow — not even any juices.

The only thing that could make this scene worse was if I suddenly transformed into a naked woman.

I dragged the body away from Connor. Noise made me look up. I saw Connor peeking out from his snow dome, staring at me, eyes wide, a Glock in his hand.

*If that asshole shoots me... well... he'd just better not.*

I kept dragging the body and, after a time, Connor disappeared back into his shelter.

I'd moved it 300 yards from Connor when I heard movement in the trees. The pack was coming.

Oh boy.

My heart sped up. I was in unknown territory here. Would the wolves eat a human? They almost never attack them. In the last two centuries, only two wolves have attacked a human without being provoked.

But meat is meat.

As for how they'd react to me... these past two days were the first time I interacted with wild wolves, so I had book knowledge but absolutely no street smarts.

From everything I had read, this meeting could go either way. Peace or all-out war.

And... all that assumes Connor doesn't try to shoot us all — me included.

I sat down, equal distance from the body and from Connor. Both were dangerous to me.

If I had to pick one job that I considered the worst job in the universe — it would be a diplomat. I'd hate every second of it and, honestly, I would suck at it. My tolerance for people's sniveling little spats and self-serving justifications is non-existent at best.

Yet, here I was.

On the one hand, I had to convince a pack to take a meat gift and ignore the wolf and the human camped right in the middle of their territory.

At the same time, I had to stop a wounded warrior — used to being the top dog wherever he went — from responding to a real threat.

I needed to make him trust me without doing anything that could look unnatural for a wolf.

I was sitting with my back to Connor's position. I figured he wouldn't shoot a wolf in the back. If I was wrong...

There was a tiny noise behind me and I looked over my shoulder.

Connor was watching again. He smelled strongly of blood. Both his and the dead man's.

Not good.

I badly wanted to shake my head "no" at him. Or use my paw to urge him back into his hidey-hole.

But I was hoping to get out of this complete fuckup with my secret identity still secret. And with no additional humans, or wolves, dead.

I turned back, away from Connor, towards the wolves.

And... here they came, black coats stark against the snow.

Faces, eyes, tails. They appeared and disappeared around the thick brush that ended 20 feet from the body.

Two. Four. Five. Seven. Nine. Twelve wolves. They peed and the scent danced in my nose. Parents and eight siblings from three litters. And two gray-furred outsiders the pack had allowed in. Those two stood out, although the fur of the alphas was turning a similar grey from age.

I stood up tall, a little bigger than their biggest male.

The leaders walked closer to the body.

I didn't move. They could smell me on the meat from when I'd dragged it. I was hoping they'd see it was a gift and accept it.

They snarled, claiming the food.

I didn't move. Conceding their right to it.

From the side of my eye, I caught another wolf slipping around me and towards Connor.

*Don't you dare shoot me*, I thought as I ran within ten feet of Connor then turned away from him and faced back to the approaching wolf. I raised my hackles, exposed my teeth and gave my most ferocious growl.

*Mine!* I staked my claim to Connor as strongly as I could.

Motion behind me!

Another wolf was coming in from the other side. Coming close.

I snarled and lunged at him. Then turned and lunged at the other wolf. I scooted back until my butt was almost close enough for Connor to touch.

There I made my stand.

Take the food. But despite the meat blood on him, anyone coming for Connor will die.

And I am strong enough and powerful enough to make sure it wouldn't be just one of you dead.

This was not my favorite option because I'd be dead too.

Wolf-on-wolf kills were the number two source of dead wolves, and I was hoping not to add to the statistics.

Humans were the number one wolf killers.

Would Connor hold it together — or would he start shooting?

I stared at the head female. It was all up to her. What would she decide?

# 32

## JUDY

J
udy was impressed. Mason got them a helicopter almost as quickly as she could have. She'd driven the switch-back US 191 in Connor's SUV rental for 35 minutes until she reached the Dailey Creek Trailhead. She left the lights on for the chopper, then turned them off as the pilot spotlighted the open area and set down in what was otherwise pitch dark.

Twenty minutes later, Judy's favorite private jet company met them in Bozeman to get them out of this heaven-forsaken state. Why anyone would live in this weather was beyond Judy.

The second snowstorm this week started just as they took off. Judy was taking Dakota to their safe house in Wichita.

In the air, Judy called the Big Sky rental company to settle up and have her things shipped to Tulsa.

Mason told her that Connor had put her cat Lola in a fancy pet boarding house where, unfortunately, she'd have to remain until it was safe for Judy to take her home.

Judy hoped this would be over in five more days — by Friday. She really wanted to ship Lola to Wichita, but... it could be noticed and give up where she and Dakota would be.

As for the girl, Dakota had followed Judy in a daze until it was time to board the plane. When Judy wouldn't tell her where it was going, Dakota twisted up her face in a stereotype of rebellion. She opened her mouth...

Judy jumped in before Dakota could talk. "Something's happening on Thursday." She saw the acknowledgment in Dakota's eyes.

"We need to talk about it. But until Friday, both of our lives are in danger. Do you really want to get caught again? Or killed?"

Dakota came in and plopped down in a seat and sulked as the plane took off. She only brightened up when they offered food.

She ate like she'd been starving.

Judy tried to recall herself at 18, and when she did she hoped like heck the girl was nothing like she'd been. The easiest way to get Judy to do something at that age was to tell her not to do it.

Oh dear!

Then she had a better idea.

She sat down across the aisle from Dakota as the girl finished a big piece of yellow cake with triple chocolate frosting.

"Sweetie, we haven't just been trying to find *you* — although you were our top priority. We're also trying to find out what really happened to your daddy."

Dakota's eyes narrowed and she said flatly, "He froze to death."

Judy shook her head. "He was murdered."

Dakota's eyes widened. "You know that? For sure?"

"He overheard a fight about money between a father and a son. Five days later, the father was dead and the son had the money. Three days after that, Otto was dead."

"Tell me who!"

"I will — as soon as we find out," Judy said. "But first you have to tell me what you know. Because the son isn't who kidnapped you. He knew about it, but he wasn't in charge. There's someone more powerful behind all of this. There's a connection between what happened 11 years ago and what's happening now."

Judy pulled out her phone and started recording.

"Tell me everything you did and found out and overheard since you got to Montana."

"I tell you everything, then you tell me everything. Right?"

"Right," said Judy.

Dakota started talking.

# 33

## WOLF-SARA

The female wolf stared at me for a very long time. I had no idea which way she would choose.

Then she snarled a final threat at me — to make sure I knew who was boss — and bent her head to eat. Her male partner joined her.

I winced when one of the yearlings snapped off an arm and ran off ten feet away to enjoy his prize. Belatedly, I wondered who the guy was and hoped he wasn't anybody so famous or important that his disappearance would cause a ruckus.

Now it was time to deal with Connor.

I turned my head and looked at him, sitting not two feet from me.

His eyes were unusually wide, he was breathing like he'd been running, and his pulse was fast. The smell of blood on him was tantalizing.

Oh boy. Dealing with him was going to be tricky.

Normally I'd just bare my teeth until he backed down.

However, playing dominance games with a scared soldier armed to the teeth — who was currently watching 12 wolves devour another man's body — well, it didn't seem too smart.

But it was hard — really hard — to lower my head to him as if I were some dog begging for scraps.

But I did it.

He froze.

It turned my stomach, but I moved my head up against his hand as if begging to be petted.

*He'd better get with the program before I was tempted to bite his hand off.*

*Okay... let's be honest. I was already tempted.*

There. I felt just the lightest touch of his hand on my head.

I leaned into his hand and he petted me. Gently. Then more firmly.

Grudgingly, I acknowledged to myself it felt good. Most important, it was working. I could hear his breathing and his heart slow down, closer to normal.

I turned my nose to his thigh, where his blood smelled the strongest. He tensed, but he let me smell. He'd been stabbed and lost blood, but he'd stopped it for now.

I leaned in against his leg and it jerked away. Funny like. Disjointed. And Connor gasped.

Now I knew why Mason sent me here. Something was torn, so Connor wasn't getting out of here on his own. Mason would be coming after the snow stopped.

Wouldn't that be fun?

He'd have to rescue the two of us separately. And we'd have to gather up all the dead man's bones. It wouldn't be smart to leave them out here.

I turned back to the pack. I smelled...

My three former pack mates had followed me here. They looked at me.

I snarled at them, rejecting them.

The two smaller wolves turned aside, but the big male stared at me for longer.

Then he turned his head to the big pack.

I held my breath.

The alpha female — her smell had told me she was his mother — stalked over to him.

He licked the sides of her mouth, and she laid her head on his shoulder. Dominant, but accepting him.

I turned to look at the alpha male — his father. If he disagreed...

He walked over to join his mate. The son lay down in the snow but did not roll over. His father stood over him for a few seconds, then turned and went back to eating.

A fist that I didn't realize had clenched around my heart suddenly eased up. All three of them were accepted into the pack. They might leave again in the future, but for now they were safe.

Later, the wolves melted back into the trees and I was alone with Connor. I watched him get as comfortable as he could in the tiny lean-to.

Figuring he needed the warmth, I snuggled my butt up against him, leaving my head facing out — where I could hear any trouble coming towards us.

I liked Connor's odor around me. It smelled of friend and ally. Although... my nose wrinkled as I thought of his blue briefs dropping from the sky onto my nose. I shook my head to chase the image away, tucked my head down and fluffed my tail over my nose.

My human mind tried to worry about the case and what had to be done next. My stomach growled in hunger, although there was nothing I could do about that now.

Connor turned on his com system and my wolf ears could hear Mason through his earpiece.

"...you okay?" I heard.

"I'm fine for now," Connor said.

"No wolves...?"

"Say again."

"All wolves ... still alive?"

"Yep. In fact, you won't believe this but I got a wolf right here, in my shelter with me. It seemed determined to protect me from the others."

"Good."

"Mase, I reckon you'll find an abandoned electric snowmobile when you come for me. Don't know how much battery will be left — given the cold."

"Thanks, I'll look for it."

They said their good nights, then Connor turned off the com.

I listened to him fall asleep, reminded myself we were both safe — for the moment — and drifted off myself as more fat snowflakes fell over the land.

# 34

SARA

I woke up to Connor petting me — not something I'd ever imagined.

Or ever wanted.

It felt really good, which I found disturbing enough to get up and go outside to pee. The sky was light pink with dawn, and the snow had stopped earlier than expected. It was going to be a beautiful day.

Connor turned on his com and talked to Mason about his leg. I could hear him say he thought one of his tendons had been severed.

Mason said they'd pick him up in a helicopter in less than an hour and that Judy would find him the best doctor in Tulsa.

Mason spoke a little louder as he told Connor that Judy and Dakota were at our safe house, and Dakota was telling everything she knew.

Silly man. He didn't have to talk louder for me to hear.

I looked back in as Connor finished his bottle of water, then started fumbling with his pants. Before I realized what he was doing, he was peeing into the bottle.

Something I would have to work to un-see.

The chopper arrived, and I backed away while the pilot and Mason got Connor strapped in.

Mason pulled two bags — one big enough to be a bodybag —

from the chopper. He told Connor they were flying him to the plane in Bozeman, then coming back.

"I want to clean up this place," he said.

Connor nodded, but he kept staring at us as the chopper lifted up and took him away.

Connor's quizzical look was no surprise — Mason had been staring at me the whole time he was down here. It was noticeably weird and it puzzled Connor.

It would have puzzled me in his place.

Once the plane was out of sight, Mason sat down hard and put his face in his hands.

*Oh hell.*

I tried to think of the last few days as Mason had experienced them, and I found myself feeling guilty.

I walked over to him, stuck my snout under his arms and pushed him backwards onto the snow. He reached for me and grabbed me tight, squeezing me until I couldn't breathe.

I waited for him to stop, but he didn't. I really needed to breathe, so I stuck out my tongue and licked all over his face.

Fortunately, he let go. He was laughing, but his eyes were red. I came back and nuzzled him.

Best. Friend. Ever.

He jumped up and opened one of the bags. Inside was a sealed baggie with... oh, thank you, Jesus... four raw steaks. I grabbed the entire baggie and ran into the lean-to.

I didn't think for a second anyone had a drone watching us, but I wasn't taking any chances.

I ripped open the bag with my teeth and swallowed each steak while my stomach cried tears of joy. I barely tasted them as they went down.

Right before the pain of transforming started, I felt an odd moment of regret.

The life I could have led here in Yellowstone.

I mean... I didn't really... I wanted my Sara life back. It's just... well... there was a feeling I had when being a wolf was all I knew. A feeling of rightness... of knowing my place in the world... of life without all the questions and the complications.

A natural life one could just live without overanalyzing it.

Once I was human, I lay on the pine branches, panting from the pain and relieved to feel it disappear. My stomach growled and I realized I was still starving. I was also lying there buck-naked and cold. I looked up, and Mason had plopped a pile of clothing for me by the opening.

Delighted, I found thick, wooly socks and snow boots, sweat pants and a long-sleeved t-shirt. Plus a sweater and a parka. And gloves! And all in my sizes. I got dressed, went out to see Mason and gave him a hug.

"Thank you. You're the best friend ever."

"And best partner?"

"Best everything!"

"In that case," Mason dug around in the same bag and pulled out a sealed bag with three Big Macs with everything except the pickles.

I nearly swooned. He even brought me two cans of Diet Coke.

I thought, *This man is going to make a wonderful husband to some lucky woman someday.*

Then I shut off my brain and ate.

Tummy full, I wrinkled my nose at him. "Did you have to use Connor's underwear?"

His face twitched like he wanted to laugh. "You wouldn't respond to your name. I wanted the strongest odor I could get."

I wrinkled my nose.

"Whatever works — right?"

"I guess."

We spent the next hour digging all around where the man's body had been. We found both femurs, his skull, his arms... in fact, everything except one rib and some finger bones which had probably been eaten. They all went into the black, waterproof bag that did not look like a bodybag but which really was one.

The pilot called with a 20-minute ETA for his return. It gave us some time to catch up.

"How long have I been missing?"

"Three days."

I nodded. "That's what I thought. What did you tell Connor and Judy?"

"That you were undercover and couldn't be contacted."

"You ran things those three days. Maybe you should do it more often?"

"I'll quit if I ever have to do it again."

I looked at him. He was deadly serious.

"Oh, you poor thing," I said, oozing fake sympathy and patting him on the back.

He looked at me and scratched his cheek with his middle finger.

God, I'd missed him.

"So... where are we on the case? Before I got shot I told you that Rasmussen wasn't the top dog in all this, didn't I?"

"Yes. We also know something is happening in three days. They were holding Judy until then. She overheard one of her jailers saying they could kill her on Friday. Plans for Dakota may have been the same."

"Advice?"

"Well... technically our case is over. We found Dakota and rescued her."

I laughed.

He joined me. "Yeah, well, I figured you wouldn't leave it like that."

"I don't think we can. If we do nothing, Dakota is still not safe. If they were going to kill her — and Judy — on Friday, they will still be planning on it."

I heard the noise of the returning helicopter. Mason and I had everything packed in his two bags, so the chopper was only down for a minute before we were airborne.

The noise as we flew was painful to my ears. Mason got us headsets but gave a look to the cockpit as he handed me mine. No private conversations.

I looked out over the land I'd so recently been a part of, seeing what I thought was the territory I'd staked out with my new pack.

Mason interrupted my thoughts with a touch to my shoulder. He fidgeted, looking uncomfortable.

"Spit it out," I said.

"I need to go back to Tulsa. My mom's having surgery tomorrow morning."

"Oh, jeez. Of course. Go."

"And I can check on Connor's surgery. And I can still do research. I don't have to be here."

"I'll need you on coms — Wednesday latest. It's best if we can solve this by that night because we don't know the timing of what's supposed to happen on Thursday."

Bozeman Airport came into view.

Mason said, "I've got a plane leaving in an hour. And I reserved you an SUV."

"Thanks, partner."

We jumped off the chopper and went into the terminal.

Before we parted in separate directions, Mason said, "Call Judy. She needs to hear from you."

# 35

## SARA

"You disappeared on us!" was the first thing Judy said to me. "Hot sex with some hunky guy?"

That was Judy.

"I wish," I told her.

"Here's an idea," she said. "Next time, wait until *after* I'm rescued before you go catting."

I shook my head. "It seems like you did great without me. Maybe I should disappear more often."

"Don't even joke about that."

"I missed you, too, Judy. Now what have you got for me?"

I heard a big, exaggerated sigh.

"Here's what I already know," I said. "Mason told me we're looking at a Big Sky ranch named Lodgepole Sanctuary. There are no regular audio or video dumps going out from the house, so if it's a blackmail scheme — it's a targeted one, not broad.

"Since Mason still can't find who the owners are, he said you're looking at frequent guests. Also, something's happening on Thursday — in three days. What else you got?"

"Okay," Judy said. "Dakota was cleaning the walk-in pantry in that house when she overheard two men talking about waiting for a vote to happen on Thursday. She wasn't paying much attention, but she noticed when the conversation stopped, almost in mid-sentence. Then a man ducked his head into where she was and looked at her. He asked her name and she told him. Something about him asking her name worried her. But he told her to carry on and left. She didn't hear the voices again. Two days later, she's snatched."

"Who was the man?"

"She didn't know. Not even a first name. So I showed her all the photos I've found of people who've been staying in that house, and... we found him!"

I grinned. "Of course you did."

"His name is John J. Andersen, but he goes by J.J. He's a Senior Vice President at KDRP Oil & Gas, one of the 10 biggest energy companies in the world. I found a picture of him with the CEO, a guy named Augustus Kingsley, and another one five years ago with Al Rasmussen.

"And... here's the most interesting thing. J.J. is on the board of Explorer Estates. It's a holding company that owns the most exclusive rich-people communities in the world. Places where the mega rich can live and dine and recreate — all without having to step out of their enclaves and mix with the rest of us scummy, ordinary people. Explorer Estates owns the Shining Peak Club in Big Sky, where this ranch is, and 30 more communities all around the world."

She'd tumbled that out almost too fast for me to process it.

"And..." she added, "J.J. is also a frequent guest at one of the other Explorer Estates' enclaves named Enchanted Rock Club. Which is in Texas."

"That's all you got?"

"What??? Are you kidding me?"

"Yes, I am." I grinned. I so loved to push her buttons.

She sputtered.

"Don't get mad," I said. "Just think about how big a raise I'm going to owe you."

"You bet your sweet patootie you will."

I had no answer for that. "Any luck on finding what happens Thursday?"

"Not yet. But now that we know KDRP Oil is involved, I'm looking at any Montana votes coming up that relate to oil and gas. Give me a couple of hours."

I thought about how I could use this information. "Judy, I may need a drug to make other guests at that house sleep. You told me you were working on a prescription drug source?"

"Ooh, I got the sweetest source. The guy's a teddy bear. Just tell me what you want. I'll tell you if he can't get it."

"Something that will knock out people fast and keep them out for six hours. Enough for six people. If there's more than that, I'll be screwed anyway."

I added, "Also, if you get a chance, I'd love a confirmation that J.J. is staying at that ranch right now."

"I'll try. Talk to you soon."

"Wait. How's Dakota?"

"She's shaken but very determined to help us prove her father was murdered. She also had a long chat with her mother last night."

"I'll call you in 2-3 hours. And, Judy? Good work!"

Two hours later I was looking at pictures of the ranch on Google Earth when Judy called back.

She said, "There's a vote at the Montana Energy Board on Thursday afternoon. They're voting on protecting water rights for energy companies, especially for fracking. That's a big thing these days. Our groundwater reserves are shrinking fast, and oil companies want to head off any attempts to start controlling the gazillion gallons of water they can take and ruin."

"Ruin?"

"Once they use it for fracking, it's poisoned with radiation and can't be used by humans or cattle or farming."

I heard her take a deep breath. "Sara, there's a bigger problem. Dakota's mother is missing."

"Seriously missing?"

"Dakota says her mother got real quiet when Dakota told her about being kidnapped. Today, Emily's phone is set to go automatically to her voicemail. Dakota called her neighbors and they say she left last night in her car. Dakota thinks she's going to confront somebody. You think it might be the guy who was sending her checks? That attorney in Houston?"

"Good idea. I'll talk to Mason about it. Meanwhile, what do we do about your security for the next three days?"

There was a pause. Then Judy said, "You mean because of her call to her mother? I had her call on the plane, not here... but... you're right. She called again from here. So if they're tracking her mother's phone..."

"See if you can't get a couple of bodyguards from the firm Connor works for. Call him and get his advice on who. Or, if they don't have anyone, he can tell you who else to contact. Do it quick."

"On it." She hung up.

# 36

## SARA

I apologized to Mason who had barely gotten off the plane in Tulsa before I needed him.

But time was critical.

He tracked Emily's phone last night through two calls she'd made. The last one was at three A.M. to AJF Insurance in Houston, the place that had been sending her retirement checks. The triangulated cell towers said she was right at the address when she called. An answering service picked up.

The service called another number, then that number called a man named William James. He was a sweetheart of a guy who'd served time as a juvie for assault, then graduated to murder 15 years ago. He got out of prison after serving 13 of those years.

Mason got his home address. We lucked out that he was renting a house, not an apartment.

"It doesn't look good," he told me. "Three hours after James got the call, Emily's cell phone SIM card was pulled and her service was disconnected. The phone likely has a new owner already."

"You think she's dead."

Mason's silence said everything.

"But she could still be alive?"

"It's *possible.*"

I shook my head. I didn't like Emily from the moment I met her. And I resented her distracting me from what was going to happen on Thursday. However...

"I'm going to Houston to make sure. I'll catch the next plane to Tulsa, then drive my truck down there."

I wanted my own wheels so I'd leave no paper trail that I was ever in town.

"But..."

"I can take up to 36 hours and still be back in Bozeman on Wednesday."

I nodded. "Thanks, Mason. I'll handle this one on my own. Go be with your parents."

"Don't be ridiculous. I'll work it with you."

"You need to be with your mother," I said. "This is an easy one."

"You need me."

"Not for this one. You need a break."

"Sara..."

He was annoying me. "You know, I did okay before I met you. In fact, I rescued your ass all by myself."

I could almost picture him rolling his eyes.

"Don't roll your eyes, you know it's true."

"You got us both shot."

"You didn't get shot."

"I would have if the bullet didn't hit my laptop first."

"Like I said, you weren't shot."

He stared at me. "You're determined?"

I nodded.

"I'll keep my phone nearby in case you run into trouble."

I turned and stalked out the door.

*When did he start thinking I was incompetent without him?*

I napped on the plane, then had a seven-hour drive to Houston. I got there in time to rent a room and have a late dinner.

At 11 P.M., I was in South Houston. When I Googled the area, let's just say they didn't rate it as one of the safest places to be.

Willy James' house was next to several like it — none of them had landscaping or even a flower box. They all had carports instead of garages, so I could see he wasn't home.

I parked three blocks away at a gas station — just in case things got hairy.

It was easy even for me to pick Willy's door lock. I planned to wait for him to return, but when I saw the inside of his place, I hoped that would be soon. The less time I was in that cesspool, the better. He had trash everywhere. Dirt and smears I did not want to investigate. I was sure there were cockroaches under some of his many piles of junk.

I was so glad I was wearing black nitrile gloves.

And the odor! When I'm in wolf form, most odors are interesting. Feces, for example. You wouldn't believe all the things you can learn about an animal or a person from smelling their poop. It's amazing — and wonderful!

As a human... the stink of this place made me want to throw up.

I found a kitchen chair that looked the least horrific of any flat surface in the place, and I sat on it. And sat. And sat.

Four hours later, when I finally heard his car drive up, I wanted to punch him just for living in such a pigsty.

I waited for him on the side of the door that opened in. Many people think you should wait on the other side of the door, where you'll be hidden as the door swings in front of you.

Getting to someone from that side is slow.

If you wait where I did, 95% of the time their face will appear almost next to you, and one of their hands is likely to be out of commission on the door knob.

Where's the best place to hit someone for maximum impact when you have surprise on your side? Theoretically, go for under the jaw — you snap back the head and you might knock them out. You're at least guaranteed they won't be able to think straight for a second or two.

The downside is you will likely break your knuckles.

Been there. Done that. No thank you ever again.

Because my right arm was against the wall, I used my left to punch him in the diaphragm — as hard as I could.

It wasn't hard enough.

His jacket, shirt, and something in the jacket pockets blunted the blow. He also had superior reflexes and had moved back slightly.

I grabbed his shoulders and threw him into the room.

Pain exploded in my side.

I saw him lying on the floor, blood glistening from a knife he held.

My blood.

I kicked the door shut and pulled my Spyderco knife from my ankle holster.

He hesitated.

His eyes even glanced down towards his waist where I suspected he had a pistol. He wouldn't be out without one — not in Texas. The only question was whether it would be in a holster — the only legal hoop required here for carrying a gun.

But he looked at me and saw female. To him that meant he didn't need the gun. That it would be much more fun to use the knife on me.

He eased up to his feet and we faced each other.

Willy James had four inches on me and was uglier than his mug shot. He'd added tattoos that covered him from the top of his t-shirt to right under his jaw. Stubble and a scraggly mustache looked like they grew up from the tats.

Willy smiled.

Connor knows how to knife fight. I saw him once and it was dazzling. Me? Not a chance. My strategy, if you could call it that, was to try to stab someone before I'm stabbed.

Tonight, I'd already lost that battle.

Willy sneered and opened his mouth. I knew he was going to tell me in detail how much fun he'd have cutting me up — and I was tired, and pissed, and really not interested in hearing it.

I pulled back my arm with the knife — making myself look like an idiot who thought a big swing of the knife was the way to fight. What I was really doing was turning my body sideways so I'd have a better kick angle.

I charged at him, swinging my knife hand towards his neck. Knives make a wonderful feint — it's hard to look anywhere else when one is coming at you.

He moved his empty hand up to block my strike. His knife hand stayed right in front of him — ready for me to impale myself on it.

Instead I kicked him hard, breaking a kneecap, then using the strength of that kick to spin myself off and to the side of him.

He swallowed a cry and fell.

His hand with the knife hit the floor. One second later, I stomped on it with my boot.

And again.

And again.

Then I kicked him in the diaphragm.

Yikes!

Pulling myself together, I zip-tied his hands. I searched him and found the handgun — a Hi-Point C something — and brass knuckles. I pocketed them and his car keys.

Lying there, broken knee cap, broken wrist, and hands zip-tied, he still gave me 'the look.'

I'd seen it before on thuggish men whose job — and self-image — depend on people fearing them. Men who think they are prepared to die rather than to talk.

And some of them are.

I dragged the chair I'd waited on over to him and sat down, pulling out my phone. I found the three pictures of women I'd cued up and showed him the first.

"Did you kill this woman in the last 48 hours?" The picture was a black-haired 40-something woman that was not Emily. I'd got it off the Internet.

He frowned at me and said, "No." His smell had the tiniest whiff of fear stink.

I switched to a different picture of another dark-haired, not-Emily woman. "Did you kill *this* woman?"

"No." He rolled his eyes at me and his smell stayed the same.

I pulled up a picture of Emily Hawking and showed it to him. "Did you kill her?"

"No." He stared at me, trying to look bored — and succeeding. But his sweat glands gave him away.

"Hell." I stood up, picked up my chair and threw it against the wall, smashing it into kindling. I had known Emily was likely dead. But knowing it for sure....

I ached for Dakota — losing her father so young and now her mother. I knew almost exactly how that felt, although my father had disappeared when I was eight — worse, I think, because I always worried he'd left us on purpose.

And now her mother. I sighed. The least I could do would be to find her for a burial.

I squatted down five feet away from Willy.

"Okay," I said. "You and I both know you're lying, and you killed her. But I can't prove it, so I can't turn you over to the cops.

"All I want from you now is her body so her family can bury her."

I waited until he looked at me. "I'm not going to ask you anything that would incriminate you. Or who you work for. Understand?"

He just looked at me.

"Instead, let's talk hypothetically. Let's imagine some unknown guy in Houston who kills people for a living, okay? Let's say this unknown, hypothetical guy wanted to get rid of a body — where would he likely put it?"

He sneered. "I ain't telling you nothing."

"Gee, you don't *look* stupid. But maybe you are? I'm not asking what *you* did — only what *somebody else* might have done. Surely you hear things. Where people might dump bodies."

He said nothing.

"You tell me where somebody *else* might have dumped her body and you get to live. Otherwise? Maybe I'll stomp on your wrist again. Or your knee. And if you keep pissing me off — you wouldn't be the first asshole I've killed."

He gave me his tough-guy stare.

I gave him my look I'd worked on in a mirror. A look that said he was annoying me and I might really enjoy killing him. It's even more convincing when you mean it, like I did right then. You have to do something with the eyes — let them go bleak and empty like nobody lives there.

He saw that darkness in my eyes and looked away, swallowing. Then he looked back and me and said, "Hyporetically?"

I nodded. "Hypothetically."

"Probably out in the desert. Nobody around for miles."

I looked at him and smelled him. The fear stink didn't increase, but there was a lot already in the room. His heartbeats didn't change either. He wasn't afraid to talk about local deserts.

"On the other hand," I said, "you'd have to drive for miles to get to an empty desert. And the land around here is flat. People can see long distances. Where else might they leave a body?"

He shrugged. "The news says some bodies were found in bayous here." He looked casual, but I heard his heartbeat speed up.

"Hmm... tell me the name of just one of the bayous you heard in the news. Where bodies were found."

He frowned. "One?"

"You said some bodies were found in bayous — plural. Just tell me one of the bayous mentioned."

He shrugged. "Okay. The Buffalo Bayou."

"Now tell me one more."

He frowned harder. "The Sims."

"Now tell me another."

"The Brays."

And there it was again. The increase in heart rate.

"I have an idea," I said. "Let's go visit the Brays Bayou!"

I reached down and grabbed him by the zip ties to drag him to the car.

He screamed. *Oh, yeah, that broken wrist.*

I grabbed him by the neck, leaving space so I didn't choke him, and with my right arm only lifted him up off the floor.

I stared at him.

His eyes darted around. "How are you doing this? Women can't..." he gasped.

"I am the angel of death," I said, very careful not to smile. I also couldn't show how hard it was to hold him up like this. Any second, my arm would give out.

"Want more proof?" I asked, dumping him to the floor — on his butt — just as my arm was about to drop him anyway.

"Look." I showed him the bloody hole in my jacket and my t-shirt.

Then I pulled them up and showed skin that had just the faintest line of red where the blade had been. "Another minute and I'll be completely healed — from a knife that went in at least two to three inches."

I waited as he considered that.

"I've come for Emily Hawking. I need her body."

"You're no angel."

"Maybe I'm the devil? I can change my body however I want. Like this..." I let my mouth and nose elongate, fusing, turning into a snout.

His eyes got huge, and he used his heels to scoot away from me. He cried out as he felt his broken kneecap, but his other foot kept scooting, backing him up.

I moved towards him, opening my jaws and displaying all my 42 gleaming, long fangs. He whimpered and shut his eyes as I spread my jaws, enclosing his face and head. I held the position, teeth holding him in place, digging in enough to draw a little blood — knowing that eventually he'd have to open his eyes.

I wanted him to see an up-close vision of my tonsils.

When I heard a whimper, I knew I'd won.

Finally I pulled back.

His eyes were frozen on me, his heart hammering, his breathing ragged.

I cocked my wolf head at him. As if asking him a question.

He said, "Whatdaya want?"

Slowly I morphed my face back to human. His eyes were glued to me.

"I want the body of Emily Hawking. It's my job. I have to take her."

I stared at him. "And I'll do whatever it takes to get her. Anything it takes. Understand?"

He nodded.

# 37

## SARA

I stood up and grabbed Willy James by his jaw, flipped him on his back, and dragged him out of the house. I unlocked his shiny, new Ford F-150. It was the Super Snake Lariat version, which I happen to know cost him well over $100,000.

I opened the passenger door and looked inside. The sight of McDonalds and Taco Bell food wrappers on the floor made me shake my head. He was well on the way to turning his $100K truck into a pigsty like his house. I opened the glove box and was not surprised to find another handgun. And another in the console between the seats. I pocketed both of them and leaned over to feel under the driver's seat. Yep. Another one there.

My pockets were full.

I lifted him up and into the passenger seat. I put another zip tie through the one holding his hands and fastened it around the passenger door armrest.

Using my phone, I got the coordinates to drive to Brays Bayou, which turned out to be 31 miles long. I wanted to make sure he wouldn't give me bad directions.

"What do I put in the GPS to get there?" I asked. "Where her body will be."

"Mason Park."

We were right in the middle of Houston when Willy had me turn into Mason Park, then drive past the soccer field. We parked just where the bushes stopped, which was farther from the water than I wanted.

It turns out the "bayou" was really a concrete channel for floodwater, with wide banks on each side that quickly dropped down to a deeper channel. Right now, only the deeper channel was filled with water. The wide concrete banks must be to accommodate four to five times the water when it rains.

It was the dead of night, in the middle of an unlighted park, but the surrounding city lights made everything visible. Still, with my black clothes and dark hair, I was unlikely to be seen.

Probably.

"How deep is that center channel?"

"Here, it's three to four feet."

"Where is she?"

He nodded his head at the path on the opposite bank that dead-ended at the bayou. "Right across from that path."

"How fast is this water?"

"Slow. And a cinder block is holding her down."

I stared at him. "If she's not there…"

"I never moved her."

I checked his arms, then reconsidered and added another zip tie that fastened one of his ankles to a bar under the seat. I didn't worry about him yelling — nobody could be that stupid.

I kept my head down as I moved to the bayou because skin is a beacon at night and also because Homeland Security money has caused most city police departments to go crazy with cameras.

They're everywhere.

Keeping the dead-end path on the opposite bank lined up, I slipped down into the dry concrete outer channel and walked down to where the water started. I could see a drop-off there, but the water was too murky to see more than an inch or two down.

I hesitated, imagining what was in the water. Trash, scum, all the chemicals people put on their lawns, and anything people think is too toxic to put in their trash. Maybe turpentine.

And dead bodies. Apparently multiple dead bodies.

The water in the deepest channel was about 15 feet across. If it really was just three or four feet deep, I could walk around in it, searching for a body with my feet.

Wincing, I went in. The first step brought water up over my knees. The second step took me down to my waist.

I reasoned Willy wouldn't have liked this any more than I did, so he probably stood next to the water and hurled the body as far as he could throw it. It should be close to this bank.

Turning to my left, I walked along about three feet from the rise, swinging my feet out to each side. Searching for Emily.

The first time something alive touched me in the water, I nearly screamed. It was a fish. I couldn't believe there were fish in here. If they could live in this muck, then so could other things.

Like snakes.

I scrunched my eyes closed and kept moving.

After 20 yards in that direction, I turned back and retraced. Then I kept moving past where I'd started.

I was about to quit and go beat up Willy for lying when the toe of my left foot moved into a hole in something hard and was trapped. My body was moving forward and I lost my balance. I flailed my arms, but with my foot stuck, I fell.

I splashed, landing face-first in the water.

And there she was.

Long, dark hair flowed away from her in the direction of the slow current. Her body trailed after it. Her beautiful Native jewelry was gone. Her shirt showed patches of white but was splotched with black slime.

Everything was anchored by a concrete block — the thing that had tripped me.

Sputtering, I jumped to my feet. My stomach roiled, and I tried frantically to rub the disgusting water from my face, only to see it was all over my gloves as well.

I had nothing to clean myself with that wasn't slimy. My stomach spasmed in dry heaves.

Focus!

I tried to use my feet to move the concrete block up out of the water, but I couldn't budge it up such a steep slope. Squeezing my eyes and mouth tightly closed, I reached back under the water and grabbed it, hefting it up the lip and onto the dry part of the channel.

Then I sat down on the dry concrete and pulled Emily's body up as well.

Up and out of her watery grave.

I shivered.

I brushed back her hair and saw open eye sockets. Fish had been eating her. I leaned forward and managed to get my head out over the water before I threw up. And threw up more.

Throw-up had to carry DNA, right? I couldn't leave it here for cops to find.

It was time to get out of here, but.. I sat a little longer. Feeling sick. Feeling the waste of a woman's life.

I didn't much like Emily Hawking, but she didn't deserve to die.

The wind blew lightly into my face. That's my excuse for what happened. No smell came to me from behind.

Every big city makes noise, even in the dead of night. Houston was worse, as some industrial machinery was at work maybe a quarter mile downriver. If you could call this abomination a river.

Machines were straining. Even so...

The only warning I got — or at least the only one I noticed — was a disturbance in the air. Wind coming at me from behind. Against the breeze.

I ducked down as something heavy connected with my shoulder. It smashed a couple of bones. I screamed.

Willy James had fallen to the ground right beside me with that swing of... a tire iron.

"Well, well," I said through gritted teeth. "You're not as dumb as you pretended to be."

I nodded at him. "And you're tough." He'd wrapped a shirt around his cracked kneecap — but I admired how far he was able to get on it.

And he'd broken the zip ties. I needed to figure out how he did that.

He tried to get to his feet, but his knee wouldn't cooperate. Instead he lay there. That swing of the tire iron had been his only shot.

"I saw you face plant in the water," he said. "There's brain-eating amoeba in there. You're going to die horribly."

He grinned.

Police sirens! Nearby. Someone must have seen and called it in?

Shit!

I stomped on his knee, then grabbed my knife and slit his throat. I'd leave him here, beside his victim.

Quickly, I grabbed his guns and brass knuckles from my pockets and threw them down beside him.

Too close! I could see cop car lights pulling into the park. Only the soccer field was between us. They'd see me soon.

I had nowhere to run but into the water.

Brain-eating amoeba??

I turned downriver, which I knew was East, and — blessing my luck that he'd hit my shoulder, not a leg — I ran on the concrete beside the water as fast as I could. I had maybe ten seconds before they would be at the bayou.

Ten seconds got me 120 yards away. Yes, in human form I am a tad faster than Usain Bolt's world record speed.

I disassembled my Ruger LC9 as I ran and stuffed the pieces in my pockets, except for the barrel. I'd need that.

At 10 seconds, I shoved the barrel of the gun in my mouth — not something I ever expected to do.

I dove into the water, my face screwed up in distaste. I could already taste bile in my mouth and feel my stomach spasm.

I wanted to cry.

With all my heart I wished I was back in Yellowstone Park with my pack.

Why was I doing this job, anyway?

And... oh hell... admit it.

I wanted to have Mason in my ear like normal. Mason, who could have warned me about cops before it was too late. Before I had to jump into water with brain-eating amoeba.

I had to open my eyes in this shit. I had to swim on my back, just under the water. The barrel I was breathing through was just a hair over three inches, which meant I had to watch carefully to stay as far under the water as I could, without water going into the gun barrel and thus into my lungs.

My lips squeezed tight around the tube so I could use my hands at my sides to help me move quicker. The current helped, but I wanted to go faster.

I couldn't kick because of the danger of splashing. Something that could be seen.

The bayou meandered, then turned sharply to the north.

My eyes kept moving from the water's surface to both sides, looking for fish. I'm normally an animal lover, but if one of them came near my eyes, he was going to die.

I took a minute to be thankful there were no sharks in the bayou.

At least I hoped not.

A murky blob had been moving with me for awhile, down by my left foot. Then it came closer, swimming along by my knees.

It was a catfish. A big sucker. Over two feet long.

I can recognize just two types of fish. Rainbow trout, from my days living in a Colorado cabin, and catfish — because of the funny whiskers they have.

I stopped moving my hands.

It moved closer up my body. And closer.

I waited until it was next to my fingers, then I grabbed at it and shoved it away from me. Hard.

Pain exploded in my left shoulder where the tire iron had hit. I screamed, the gun barrel falling from my mouth. I grabbed frantically for it, almost lost it, then clinched it so hard that I felt — and heard — a knuckle pop.

I swallowed water.

Retching and gasping for air, I stood up in the channel. The water came up to my armpits.

I looked desperately around, then heaved a sigh of relief that I was not in sight of where I'd been.

I frowned. The fish I'd hit was hard, not soft as expected. It had something on its back that didn't feel like scales or fins. It felt like dinosaur-armor plating on its topside.

Oh crap — there were mutant-armored catfish living in this water.

The industrial machine noises were much closer now. Where machines worked, humans were likely to be.

With reluctance, I blew air through the gun barrel and put it back in my mouth.

I lay back down in the water and continued on.

Mason would be laughing his head off at me now.

Face it, I told myself. All your loner instincts aren't working anymore. You're better with your team.

The feel of the water current changed.

I risked a quick glance and saw another bayou was joining this one. Just before it did, a small channel turned off to the right. It led through a bunch of machinery — the source of the noise I'd heard before.

I turned into the smaller channel.

To get out of this water, I needed to find a vehicle. If I called a cab while coated in all this muck, I would stick in the driver's memory — if he'd even let me into the cab.

I needed to disappear from this bayou without a trace. Which meant I needed to find a car to borrow. And where better than at some kind of industrial operation?

And no, I wasn't calling any of the team — it would be too embarrassing.

I slid past two barges parked by the bank, then the building itself. Then I put my feet on the bottom and kept walking with my head just above the black water level until I saw parked cars ahead.

One of the pickup trucks had left a window down, just waiting for me to borrow it. But I felt guilty as I sat on the seat, squishing water and gunk all over it.

Even my gloves oozed out water when I squeezed them around the steering wheel.

I drove five miles before I was able to breathe easily. At a stoplight, I pulled out my iPhone with crossed fingers.

It worked! I wanted to kiss the thing, but — hey — brain-eating amoeba.

I reached into the glove compartment and found an insurance card with George W. Jefferson's name and address. I took a picture of it because I needed to send the guy some money so he could clean all the stink I was leaving.

I left the borrowed truck in front of the house next to Willy's, then walked three blocks to my own truck. Sitting on the seat, I wondered if I would need to rip out the upholstery entirely to get rid of the water, the smell, and the germs.

Once inside my motel room, I moved straight to the shower and got in fully clothed. Everything I took off got tossed in the sink. Later, I'd bag it and then burn it when I got home.

I soaped and scrubbed myself raw. I didn't put soap in my eyes, but I ran the shower over my open eyes for hours.

Only after that did I dare to transform.

Which should take care of any brain-eating amoeba.

I hope.

# 38

## MASON

**M**ason hated hospitals.

It was bad enough dropping in on Connor and seeing him laid up, unable to move. He looked so vulnerable. Mason didn't like Connor looking helpless — it reminded him that even Connor could die.

He hated even more waiting around for hours with his dad as they removed his mom's thyroid gland and looked for signs the cancer had spread.

Oh, hospitals had gotten better at dressing themselves up. "Putting lipstick on a pig," his mom would call it. There were cushioned chairs, soft colors and even a "status screen," like for airport arrivals, that let you know the status of operations.

He could see when his mom was in the operating room. He could see when she was moved to post-op.

Still, the places were soul-suckers. They tore away your pretense of immortality and pummeled you with the recognition that we were all going to die. Something we did our best to forget. Or, at least, ignore.

Sitting in the waiting room, Mason had a vision of himself, his dad, and everyone walking around as meat like that guy the wolves ate. Meat enclosed in a bag of skin and waiting for the day the refrigeration failed and the meat would rot.

Good grief — that was morbid even for him.

He got up and helped himself to another cup of coffee. It tasted like stagnant water, but he needed the caffeine. What he really needed was to sleep for about 24 hours to recover from the past few days.

But that wasn't likely to happen.

He pulled out his secure phone and texted Sara. There was no answer.

"Everything okay?" his dad asked.

Mason looked at him, seeing someone as frayed as he was. His dad had bags under his eyes, and his mop of brown hair was more mussed than normal.

"Yeah," he said. "Everything's fine."

"You need some sleep, Mase." His father patted his shoulder awkwardly.

Mason smiled. "You too." He hesitated, then said, "I did some research..."

His dad smiled. "Of course you did."

"Why thyroid cancer? Mom's too young to get it."

His dad frowned. "She didn't talk to you about this?"

"About what?"

His dad sighed. "I told her to talk to you... well... I guess I'll tell you. You need to know for yourself. For any kids you might have."

"What?"

"When your grandmother was a young girl, she visited relatives among the Mescalero Apaches in southern New Mexico. She was there when the government tested the first nuclear bomb. She told your mom she thought it was beautiful — ashes fell from the sky for days. The kids played in them. The government said it was completely safe."

"I never knew her."

"She died in her late 20s, a year after she had your mother. She died of thyroid cancer."

"But she was just a kid when the test happened. It's not like she was pregnant with Mom."

"Of course not. Your grandmother was only 12 in 1945."

"Then why would Mom...?"

"It didn't just kill off those who were there. It did something to their genes. Generations who followed have been getting cancers. Women in their 20s or 30s. Your mother was lucky to get into her 40s."

"Women?"

"Women are three times as likely to get thyroid cancer as men."

"So I'm likely safe?"

"Don't assume that — men can get it. Get tested every three to five years. And think hard about ever having a daughter."

"Sonofabitch! Is anyone trying to fix this? Figure it out?"

His dad snorted. "The government won't even acknowledge it, much less try to fix it. They paid some money to the victims of the second test in Nevada, but they're still ignoring victims of the first test. There were 13,000 people living within 50 miles of the detonation. Mostly Native Americans. It's hard not to believe that's why they are still being ignored, even today."

A doctor appeared asking for "Mr. Spencer?" Mason and his dad got up.

"The operation went fine," he told them. "It had spread to her neck lymph nodes, but not further. That gives her a great chance for a nice, long life."

"I'm a mathematician," said his dad. "Give me the 5-year survival numbers."

"Seventy-seven percent when the cancer only spreads to one other organ. She's lucky we caught it when we did."

"Thank you."

"She should be awake in about an hour. Then you can see her. Don't let her talk much — her throat will be sore."

An hour later, after sitting beside each other with nothing more to say, they each got in to see her. She was awake and smiling to reassure them. It didn't work — surrounded as she was by machines — and looking like she was 30 years older.

His dad stayed while Mason went to the Tulsa office and passed out on the fold-out sofa. Hours later, he returned and his dad left to get some sleep. Mason sat by her bedside and held her hand.

"You scared the crap out of me. Don't do it again!"

His mom smiled. "I'm sorry," she said softly, her voice sounding like it was forced through glass shards. "For everything."

"What else?"

"The dates. How were...?"

Mason sighed. "The last two were nice. I enjoyed talking to Jisha. But no thanks — there were no sparks with any of them."

"Any girl... give you sparks?"

"Not yet, Mom."

"Hmm."

Mason frowned. "Hmm what?"

"Maybe... some girl... you not..." She started coughing.

"Stop talking Mom."

She took a sip of water. "Important," she croaked. "Maybe... your heart already picked... someone?"

"No..." Mason shook his head. Then he stopped. "Hmm... well... there was this girl in college. I thought maybe. But she moved to Alaska with her boyfriend."

"Tell me."

"She's very smart. She was in my comp sci classes, but then she dropped it back to a minor and got her major in economics. She said she couldn't sit alone all day on a computer. She needed more 'people time.'"

"And?"

"And she had this fresh-scrubbed girl-next-door look, so people didn't take her seriously. But she laughed about it. Called it her 'secret weapon.' She had a wicked sense of humor."

"Go see her. Maybe she changed her mind?"

"No, that would be...."

"Maybe she and that man broke up?"

"Hmm."

His mother cocked her head at him.

"Maybe," he conceded. "Maybe I'll check it out."

# 39

## SARA

After a four-hour nap in Houston, I drove back to Tulsa and told my car guy to do his best to clean out the stink of a fishing trip from my Ford F150 truck.

I stopped into Oklahoma Surgical to see Connor, who I thought would be driving everyone insane in his desire to get discharged early. Instead, he was deep in conversation with Lillian — my first client and his girlfriend — about new services she could add to her shooting range business. I gave her a hug and kudos for finding something to distract his mind.

Our private plane company then got me to Billings, Montana, in time for me to get an actual eight hours of sleep before I would be knee-deep in it again.

It was six A.M. Wednesday when I woke. The vote was tomorrow — so I had to get to Rasmussen first and then J.J. Andersen before then.

I ate a "Ranchers' Special" breakfast with enough sausage calories to close up every one of a human's blood vessels. It tasted delicious and I really needed the meat.

After stopping at a Dollar store to buy a wire coat hanger, I drove to where the Montana Energy Review Board meets on St. John's Avenue. I did a recon drive through their 15-car parking lot behind the building and was relieved to see Rasmussen's white Land Rover Defender 110 there.

I kept driving on out the back of the lot, then went around the block and parked in the much bigger, much-more-crowded parking lot next door.

My watch said it was 11:30, so there was a good chance Rasmussen would be leaving for lunch in the near future. I locked up my car, then moseyed over to the other lot.

I'd spent the morning wondering how best to get to the man. The easiest way I could think of was to get into his car and surprise him. I especially liked the idea because the Internet said tinted side windows were standard on his vehicle.

How would I break in? I had Judy Street to thank for my knowing how. We had five months without a client between our last case and this — and Judy decided we needed a game to keep everyone sharp. So she invented "P.I. Skills Fridays."

It was played by whoever was around that Friday — typically me, her and Connor. Sometimes Mason joined us. Judy picked the skill and we competed to see who was fastest.

Sometimes it was picking door locks, something I just couldn't seem to get. I usually came in last. Often it was drive time on an obstacle course — sometimes with a car, sometimes with a motorcycle. Connor and I were neck and neck winning those... okay, maybe he was a *little* ahead of me. And sometimes it was breaking into a car — one of Judy's specialties.

The slowest person each week — the loser — had to buy pizza and beer for the next Friday's contest.

So... getting into Rasmussen's Land Rover wouldn't be my first rodeo.

I had a fancy, inflatable bag thing back home that let me slide under a car's weather stripping and pop open doors in under a minute. Here I was forced to make do with the coat hanger. I was annoyed that it took me a full three minutes to get inside — I'd been quicker on all the other vehicles I'd tried.

I hid on the floor behind the driver's seat and waited.

The car door opened and someone got into the driver's seat. I scrunched as low as I could, expecting his bodyguard to get into the passenger seat. But Rasmussen turned on the engine and drove away — alone except for me.

I watched out the side window, and when I glimpsed a Walmart, I rose up behind him with my Ruger LC9 and said, "Pull into the Walmart, Al."

He literally jumped. I was ready to grab the wheel if I had to.

"Turn *now*, Al," I said. "I want to talk, so pull in here and park as far away from other cars as you can get."

He complied, but he looked more in the rearview mirror than where he was driving. His eyes were so wide I could see miles of white around his brown irises.

He looked like he'd seen a ghost.

As he pulled to a park, I grabbed his right arm — so he didn't get any ideas about jumping out — and levered myself into the front passenger seat.

"Where's your bodyguard?"

At his blank look, I said, "The guy with you when I met you at the lithium mine claim. I never got his name."

Al's face scrunched up like he'd tasted something sour. "His name is Freeman. But he doesn't work for me. He's just around all the time, supposedly for my 'protection.'"

"But you knew he planned to kill me — or you wouldn't be so shocked to see me now."

"He planned what? I... I don't know anything he does. I was shocked to see you because I thought I was alone."

I stared at him.

He lowered his eyes. "I did not know what he planned. But... other people have disappeared after he sees them."

I studied him. This wasn't going like I thought it would. Suddenly, I had more questions.

"Gabal Crowley," I said, naming the man who'd ordered me run off the road. "He worked for you?"

Rasmussen scowled. "He never worked for me. He was assigned to me just like Freeman."

"Your Crowley hired two goons to run me off the road not long after I got this case. I thought it was on your orders."

Rasmussen's eyes were wide. "He never answered to me."

"What happened to him?"

"I don't know. He disappeared and Freeman showed up to replace him."

"Freeman shot me that day at the lithium claim. Twice, right in the heart." I lied.

He looked at me, eyes wide, appalled but also disbelieving.

"God bless Kevlar," I added.

He nodded. "Does Freeman know you survived?"

"If he works for J.J. Andersen he knows," I said, playing a pretty safe hunch.

*Score!* Al flinched at the name.

"Two nights ago, I rescued Dakota and another woman from where he was holding them in West Yellowstone." I pretended it was me in case they didn't know about Connor.

"Apparently J.J. was holding them until your vote tomorrow. After that he was going to kill both of them."

Rasmussen didn't say anything, but his face scrunched up like he'd bit into something very sour.

I said, "I hear the vote is about something like water rights for fracking?"

Rasmussen pursed his lips and frowned. "He wants Montana to be like Texas — where oil and gas drilling don't even need a permit to drill for water to use in fracking. Did you know that fracking a single oil or gas well today uses up to 40 million gallons of groundwater? Water that is poisoned in the process so it can't be used again. They're going to kill ranching."

"Can't they treat the water?"

"It's not cost-effective. They treat maybe 15% of all the water they use. The rest of it they pump back into the ground — below aquifers. Where supposedly it won't break through and contaminate what little good water we still have. But it does break through sometimes."

I put the gun away. "It's definitely not good for ranchers."

"It's not good for anyone. Our aquifers in the U.S. are down almost a third from where they should be. With hotter temperatures, we're going to run out of water."

I frowned at him.

"We've already got millions of acres of farmland that can't be farmed because the water has dried up."

"And you have to vote for this?"

He looked away.

"What else has he been pushing?"

"Land transfer. He wants states to get as much federal land as possible."

"That's bad?"

"States are required to make the most money they can off state lands — with no consideration for whether it kills off the ecosystem. They're even required to sell it off if it isn't making money. Imagine all our public lands and pastures loaded with oil derricks and wall-to-wall fast-food joints."

I considered. "Tell me, Al, what happens if J.J. disappears? Is there someone over him who could then demand your vote?"

Al looked at me, considering. "He reports directly to Augustus Kingsley, the CEO of KDRP Oil & Gas."

"So... the question is whether his boss would keep a copy of blackmail evidence J.J.'s collected. Right?"

Al winced and looked down.

"Okay," I said. "Here's what's going to happen. Tomorrow you're going to vote against giving Montana water away to oil companies. Because if you don't — we'll release the proof we have that you killed your father."

His eyes narrowed.

I shook my head at him. "Oh, we have the proof alright. We have a recording of your fight with him the week before he died. Otto Hawking left that with an attorney we found. Plus... well... let's just say we have everything we need to put you away."

"Not much of a deal for me. It's lose/lose either way."

"So, here's how you improve your odds. I'll tell you right after I check you for recording devices."

I knew he likely had none, but I wasn't going to risk anything more on this case. I patted him down carefully. I also took off his boots and double-checked them — inside and in the heels.

When I knew he was clean, I said, "Tell me everything you know about J.J. and especially about where he stays in that Lodgepole Sanctuary ranch in Big Sky."

"And?"

"And maybe he won't be bothering you any longer."

"So what? Then I'll just have to answer to you."

I shook my head. "My job was to find and protect Dakota Hawking. You help me do that and neither I nor anyone from my firm will come after you. You and I will have nothing to do with each other going forward."

"How would I know…"

"Al, think about it. You're guaranteed to lose without this deal. With it, you have a good chance for a win."

He stuck his hand out, and I forced myself to smile and shake it. I didn't wipe my hand off on the leg of my jeans afterwards, even though I wanted to.

He asked, "What do you want to know?"

I told him.

# 40

## SARA

I f you're going to break into a house, don't drive there in a rental car. Don't even park a rental eight miles away on a deserted, dead-end road. A smart cop might wonder why the car sat there for 3 hours in the middle of the night — the exact time of the break-in. The rental companies all use GPS tracking.

Stealing a car is also a bad idea — if you have to leave the car for some time and you need it to be waiting for you when you're done. Buying a car — for cash from a private seller — is better, although not foolproof.

Google Earth showed the Lodgepole Sanctuary included a modern main ranch, small for the mega-rich — only 5,000 square feet — and a guest house.

Most important to me was that it backed up to part of the three million plus acres of the Gallatin National Forest. So instead of coming in from the east on U.S. 191 and traveling through the town of Big Sky, I was able to park my newly-purchased SUV eight miles west of the house on the Bear Creek Loop, off U.S. Highway 287.

From there, it was eight miles — all inside the forest — to the ranch.

The terrain included sharp peaks and cliff edges dropping into valleys so I estimated two hours run time for my wolf — which would get me there at one A.M.

I'd have five hours before I needed to leave the house. I could push that an extra half hour — but only if I ran full-out on the way back.

Rasmussen had told me J.J. was in town and had just dropped in on him to remind him how to vote. He had no idea how many others might be at the ranch.

I hated surprises.

It was 10:30 P.M. when I pulled off U.S. 287 at Cameron, which seemed to consist of a post office, a handful of homes with barns, and the multi-purpose Blue Moon Saloon, Cabins, RV Park, and Cafe. The RV park part of the operation was closed for the winter, and nobody was in the cabins, but the saloon had five pickup trucks parked there.

I parked beside them and checked coms with Mason.

"How's your mother?" I asked.

"The operation was fine, but she's got a 23% chance of not living five years."

"Doesn't that mean a 77% chance she does?"

"Yeah, the doc seemed to think I should be happy about that.... Wait a minute. Where are you?"

"Beautiful downtown Cameron, Montana."

"What are you doing way over... Shit — you're not going to... Sara!"

"I can't go in from the East — there are tons of people likely to see me."

"Do you know the wolf hunting situation in Montana?"

"No... but I'll be in the Gallatin National Forest."

"Give me 15 minutes to research this."

"I can't — I need to go in."

"If you're in Cameron, you still have some distance to drive. Call me again when you get to where you're leaving the car."

"Mason..."

"Call me before you change. Damnit Sara, I almost lost you once on this case. Give me time to find out what you're up against."

"Alright. I'll call again before."

It was 10:46 when I stopped at the dead end of the road that took me closest to the ranch.

I called Mason again.

The first words out of his mouth were, "You're crazy."

"Tell me."

"Montana wolf hunting season is from September 15 through March 15. Right now. And do you know Montana lets people kill 20 wolves a season? Each person can kill twenty as long as they pay Montana a fee for each wolf. Male, female, pups — they don't care. And here's something to consider. They allow nighttime wolf hunting on private property with spotlights and night vision scopes."

"But that's on private land..."

"Do you really believe someone who used spotlights to kill a bunch of wolves won't also hunt on public land and lie about it?"

"And," he added, "they can also use snares to trap and kill wolves. This is too dangerous."

Snares gave me a pause. "You're right — it's dangerous. But the vote is tomorrow."

"Screw the vote. You don't owe that Rasmussen slime bucket anything. The man killed his father for money."

"He won't get away with that."

"Look... I agree we have to go after J.J. Andersen or our client will never be safe. But we can find another way. Tomorrow or the next day."

"Mason. I just survived a bullet to the head. Granted, I never want to do that again... but still... I'm off-the-charts resilient. And this is what we do — we take down the bad guys that others can't."

He was silent.

"Mason — it's showtime. You with me?"

He sighed, long and loud. "Always."

I smiled. "Good!"

It was a human-chilly 25 degrees when I stepped out of the SUV, putting a hand-written "Car Dead — back soon" note on the windshield just in case.

I added a night scope to my custom wolf-adapted backpack and laid it out where it would be easy to wiggle into. It had to hang just right because I never found a clasp that I could reliably use with wolf paws.

The moon was out — not full, but pretty close.

My smile got wider and I let out a big sigh of contentment. Don't get me wrong, I am very grateful that I don't need to transform every full moon. That would have created serious problems in my life.

But even though it doesn't force me to transform, the moon still calls to me.

Changing under a full moon eases the pain of the first 30 seconds. Instead of swearing as my face elongates and new teeth break through my gums, I just sit there staring at the moon and feeling galaxies away from here. I hear the night come alive with all the sounds I can't hear in human form. All the missing smells come to my nose. The wind tickles as it brushes against my growing fur.

The pain only breaks through moon glamour at the end — when my spine cracks to bend the opposite direction. Then I would scream in agony, except my voice box is changing and no sounds can escape.

For a second, I wonder. Is that a mutation — not being able to scream?

I've never met another werewolf except Joe White Wolf, the man who transformed me. And he died that same day. Maybe other werewolves could scream -- so they were discovered and killed? Maybe Joe alone had the mutation that, by silencing him, protected his life?

Then I was fully wolf and I know questions like this are exactly the kind of self-indulgent, worthless crap that two-footers waste their lives with.

I slipped into the backpack, shrugged my shoulders to make it comfortable, and set out to enjoy an eight-mile run in the woods. The temperature was perfect, the moon made my path as bright as day to me, and I wanted to revel again in the feeling of being in tune with the world.

Belonging.

Except I couldn't, thanks to Mason.

Keeping my ears and nose alert for the slightest hint of hunters wasn't the problem. It was the worry about trapping that slowed me down.

Wolf eyes have just one advantage over human eyes — they are far superior at catching movement. And we're not color blind as some believe — we can see yellows and blues. Every other color looks like some shade of gray.

None of this would help me spot a trip-wire snare before I ran into it. I strained my vision, starting and stopping, trying to prevent hitting one. My stomach burned like it was full of acid.

Finally, I had to say *screw it* and just run. I could spend all night going the eight miles otherwise, and tear up my stomach with nerves. I had my teeth. If I transformed back to human, I even had wire cutters in my bag.

I just ran.

Finally, as the ground flew beneath me, I relaxed.

In my human form, I would notice the different types of pine trees — white pines are my favorites for their lacy look — as well as the underbrush and the stone formations.

My wolf barely saw them. She noticed fauna, not flora. The scent of elk that had been in that glen recently. A nest of rats living under that bush, a tree loaded with squirrels and acorns, the swish of a snake over there, an owl up there.

She noticed life.

It seemed as if just a few minutes had passed when I saw house lights — a few directly ahead and others to the right of me.

I shook my head in amusement at how easily the time had passed. And in relief that I'd encountered no snares.

I crept forward until I could make out the building directly ahead. It was an ostentatious house — like those old Southern plantations — but this one had more columns than needed to hold up a roof.

Wrong house.

I moved to my right and saw a log cabin on steroids, although it was too small for the rich to be anything but a showy guest house. Behind it was the house I'd come for. I liked the style of it, modern with a mixture of stone and wood facing, with wide, comfortable balconies overlooking the forest.

The balcony on my right was attached to the smallest of two master suites — the one I assumed belonged to J.J. Andersen. Dakota's team was allowed to clean in there only when the caretaker, a Mr. Sanders, was in the room. Otherwise they had to skip it.

I found a good spot for watching that room, back in the trees enough to hide me but with full view of the balcony, the sliding glass doors behind it, and the garage exit. I dropped my backpack there and used my teeth to open the zipper.

Inside was my comm system with Mason. I used a claw to tap the mike three times in a row so he'd know I arrived safely.

I pulled out my ATN Thor 4 thermal scope. It's meant to be attached to a rifle, but I prefer it for its high quality and for how easy it is to be held and operated when you had paws instead of hands.

I trained it on the target house and immediately saw two active fireplaces. I'd learned from Dakota and Rasmussen that this house had four fireplaces, but only two were lit now. The one in the living area was cooling, while the one in the upper left master bedroom was roaring. That was the biggest bedroom, not the one I assumed J.J. Andersen used.

Was I wrong?

I was 99% sure the bed had to be to the right or left of the sliding glass doors to the balcony. From the bed you would want to see both the view outside as well as the fireplace. I turned the scope to avoid as much of the fireplace heat as possible. It looked like two much lesser heat signatures to the left. Maybe. So perhaps a couple asleep in bed.

I turned the scope to the smaller master and saw a human-sized signature. It was not where I expected the bed to be, but it was in the room.

When I trained the scope on the lower level, I saw a diffuse signal. Perhaps it was the house heating system.

Time to take a risk instead of waiting outside and hoping J.J. would show himself.

I've broken into many houses in the three years I've been rescuing people from evildoers. I've cut holes in windows, come in with unsuspecting cleaning staff, and picked locks — although I'm pretty poor at the latter.

This time I was going to try something new — enter the code and walk right in.

Hopefully.

If they hadn't changed the code.

If I didn't have the wrong numbers.

I had two separate sources for the code. One was Al Rasmussen. The thing about having guests stay over at your house is they need the code to get into it. And if you have two or three at a time, on different dates, changing the code would be a serious pain.

Al was last at the house three months ago. He wrote the code in his iPhone notes because he kept forgetting it. He told me it was 091852.

Ideally, I'd also have the code from Mason hacking White Cleaning Services, but he still hadn't gotten into their client computer system. He told me it had to be on an isolated computer with no connection to the internet, or else he'd have it. We'd have to break into their offices if we really needed it.

Next best was Dakota. She'd cleaned the house twice a week for three months. She did not have the code, but she'd noticed the supervisor entering it. She remembered "0918" because it was almost her mother's birthdate. She didn't remember the last two numbers.

I put the scope back in my backpack and used my claw to zip it up. Then I put it behind some bushes and laid out the straps for me to easily jump into it — in case I was on the run.

I move much faster in wolf form.

The entry was on the other side of the house, so I circled around. The ground rose from back to front so that the front of the house looked like a one-story while the back of the house had two.

No cars were parked out front, but there was a four-car garage.

I was going to be totally visible for about 10 seconds getting to the front door, but it was recessed enough to hide me while I entered the door code.

If there were cameras, I'd be okay on the grounds in my wolf form. Door cameras would be a whole other matter.

I'm human-tall when I stand on my back paws, so reaching the door keypad wasn't a problem. Getting a claw directly in the center of each of the keys so it didn't slip off was a little tricky — but I was careful.

There was a second delay after entering the numbers when I was sure I'd have to sprint away. But then I heard the clank of a bolt retracting. Considerately for wolf paws, the door had a lever instead of a knob. I pushed it down and shoved the door open.

No alarms went off. I stuck my head inside and looked in all directions. A low-watt almost-night-light was on in the entry room, the only light I could see in any direction.

I waited 45 seconds, but I heard nothing.

Slowly I backed out, using my front paw to pull the lever of the door to close it.

I trotted off to the side of the house and then back down to where my backpack was. I grabbed it in my teeth and pulled it up the side of the house to a still-covered-by-trees position that was much closer to the front door.

I lay down by my bag, opened it and used my teeth to tear into two bags of wild-caught salmon. It was so good that I grabbed a third bag and wolfed it down quickly — before the pain of transformation started.

*Brrr, it was cold!*

Naked human and 20 degrees are not a good mix.

Quickly, I dressed in long underwear and a black one-piece ski suit, then added two pairs of socks and good boots. If all hell broke loose I might be on the run as a human. If so, I would rather not freeze to death.

I crumpled warm ski mittens and a ski hat and slid them inside the ski suit, then zipped it up.

My car keys and room keys went into an outside leg zippered pocket. I got my comm earpiece/mike and turned it on.

"You awake?" I asked Mason.

"Very funny."

# 41

## SARA

The door to the house had re-locked, as I had anticipated I entered the code again — so much easier with human fingers — and slipped inside.

Because J.J. would not be eager to answer my questions, I needed to make sure nobody else in the house could call security. Or the police.

Turning to my right, I checked each room, finding nobody — until I came to the biggest master suite where the fireplace was roaring and two people might be sleeping.

They were.

I checked the bathroom and closet, both of which were bigger than one-bedroom apartments in any city and much nicer as well. Nobody was hiding in them.

I eased closer to the bed. The man was jowly and ugly. The woman was a fake blonde wearing false eyelashes while she slept. They were both on opposite sides of the king-size bed.

I opened the zipper to my suit that was designed for cell phones and carefully took out two pre-loaded syringes — thanks to Judy's drug source.

He told her you can knock people out fast or you can keep them out for six hours, but getting one drug to do both was "complicated."

Instead, I used a drug they give anxious patients right before they're wheeled into the operating room. It acts almost instantly but it also dissipates quickly. Although — as if to pay me back for needing two drugs, it often caused very-short-term memory loss.

That could be a benefit.

I injected the male and then the female without either of them waking. Then I followed each shot with a sedative designed to last six hours — past daybreak when I had to be out of here.

My iWatch was set to beep me at 6 A.M.

I searched the living and other common rooms, finding nobody else. I took the stairs to the lower level, where I found a gym, one impressive media room, and two lesser bedrooms for staff.

A 40-something, muscled man who was growing a pot belly slept in one of the bedrooms, snoring so loudly it made me smile. I repeated the two injections with him, then came back upstairs.

Time to introduce myself to J.J. Andersen.

Who might be awake.

*Oh, yes, he's awake.*

I smelled him as I walked down the short hall to his suite. Or, at least, I smelled a different man than the two I'd already drugged.

The scent was strong enough that he had to have been outside his room — recently. His bathroom was inside his suite, so he would have only walked outside the door I was facing if he knew I was here. Or if he got a bad case of the munchies and went for the house refrigerator.

I was betting on the former.

I slowed my pace.

There was a door that had to be a linen closet coming up on my left, maybe seven feet from his suite door. I couldn't tell if he was in it from the smell — odors get bounced around by central heating blowers and are difficult to localize.

As I drew even with that door, I listened hard.

Nothing...

No — there it was. One inhale of breath.

I used my next step down the hall to draw me closer to the closet door.

I heard the rapid beating of a heart.

*Hello, J.J.*

I took two more steps, but they were in place — steps for the noise of them, not for distance.

I heard a big inhale of breath, and I curled against the wall, just past the door hinges.

Suddenly the door swung open. Or, at least, that was his intent.

I slammed my body against it, hitting it when it was only a quarter of the way. The door rebounded back against him as he tried to come out.

A muffled shot rang out, punching a hole through the door but well over my head and going into the roof.

I jerked the door open, looking for the gun.

It was hanging loosely in his right hand — which was touching his face where his nose was bright red and bloody.

The closet looked like a snowstorm — white pillows, white blankets and white towels. Some of them now had sprinkles of red spots on them.

I grabbed for the gun and got both my hands on it. It was slick with his blood.

His left hand punched the side of my face, just missing my temple and making me see fireworks.

I slammed my knee into his groin. He made a funny "Eek" sound and fell back against the shelves, breaking one of them. It dumped white towels all over him.

Quickly, I pulled out my trusty zip ties — never leave home without them — and grabbed his hands where they cupped his balls. Ignoring his moans, I fastened his wrists together.

I barely got it done before he flung his arms up and hit me on the bottom of my jaw. My teeth slammed together and I tasted blood from my tongue.

It hurt!

Angrily, I pocketed his gun and grabbed him by his wrists, jerking him out of the closet and onto all fours on the hall rug. It looked expensive, but he could bleed all over it for all I cared.

"Into your room," I said.

He rolled over on his butt and arched an eyebrow at me. "If you're looking for a job as a maid, you're not impressing me."

I stared at him.

"You're not pretty enough to work as one of my whores."

*Really? This was how he wanted to play it?*

"I'm better looking than anyone you could get without paying for it."

Then I reached down, grabbed where his wrists were bound, and dragged him to his door, then on into his bedroom.

I closed the door and locked us inside. The room had a beautiful wood coffered ceiling and lots of closed curtains that, during the day, would have a great view, but otherwise — meh. It was just a room.

J.J. interrupted my thoughts. "So, are we going to wait here for your boss to show up? The big guy?"

I laughed.

"J.J.," I said, walking towards him and channeling Judy, "You just keep trying, sweetie. It's cute."

I patted him on the head.

There was no way I was zip-tying his legs while he was conscious, so I carefully hit him in the throat with the side of my hand. Learning how to shut someone down for 60 seconds had often come in handy.

It's not something to try unless you don't care much if the person is seriously injured. It's hard to judge the amount of strength to use.

I zip-tied his ankles together.

And I searched him — every inch of him. I found his phone and two gadgets I didn't understand — so I just removed everything, including his watch, a ring, and his shoes. I double-checked that the phone was not recording. In fact, I pulled out the SIM card.

He came to as I was pulling off his last shoe. He tried to leverage his feet up, while they were tied together, to kick me.

It was a feeble attempt.

I shook my head at him. "Should have done more abs workouts," I said.

Then I searched his bathroom. He yelled, "Help!" Several times. I wasn't worried he'd be heard. The nearest neighbors weren't near at all and the house was very well insulated.

I'd already made sure there was no Alexa in the room, but I would have been shocked if there were. The last thing he'd want is a system out of his control recording conversations in the room.

But his yelling was annoying.

I came back into the room with a wet washcloth.

"Everyone else here is sleeping soundly for the next six hours. Your choice — I can gag you with this or you can shut up."

He stared at me, then closed his mouth.

I went back to work and found nothing in the bathroom, so I moved my search to the bedroom. There was only one painting in the room, a talented oil painting of lodge-pole pines just like those on the mountains I ran through to get here.

I pushed it to the side and there was a safe behind it.

I looked at J.J.

His face looked smug, then he wiped the look and tried instead to look concerned. Worried.

But he wasn't. His body didn't kick out even a hint of fear sweat.

I tapped the microphone part of my earpiece and said, "Is the team ready?" That's our code to let Mason know the bad guy is listening.

I used the camera I had disguised into a "Save the Wolves" pin. It was attached to my ski suit, so I pointed my shoulder at the safe.

"I don't think he's got the good stuff inside there," I told Mason. "I think it's somewhere else."

"Show me," Mason said, so I walked him through the bathroom and closet.

A year's worth of blackmail material wouldn't be taped under a drawer. It might be in a safe deposit box, but I didn't think so. It would be out of his control for hours when the bank was closed.

He'd want instant access.

Mason had me search the floor for a hidden trap door. You can't really hide the necessary cut-out on a tiled floor or hardwood, so he had me looking under rugs and under furniture. You can hide doors with a stone facade, but none of the walls or floor in his suite was made of stone.

"It's got to be in the closet," Mason said. J.J. had a custom one where everything — drawers, hangers, and shelves — are all in wall units. There was a fancy rug in the center of the room and a plush-looking loveseat on the carpet.

The room was as big as my entire cabin in the Colorado foothills.

I moved all the clothes aside, opened all the drawers and ran my fingers over every inch of it. I looked under the rug. It took forever and we found nothing.

Frustrated, I checked again on J.J., who continued to sit, acting unconcerned.

"Maybe we have to torture it out of him," I said, loud enough for J.J. to hear. "I wouldn't mind. I'm getting bored here."

"Very funny," I heard in my ear. "Gimme a second — I'm searching closet safe rooms on the internet. But all the hidden doors are shelf systems..."

I heard him inhale.

"Son of a... it's gotta be the mirror."

"The mirror?"

J.J. flinched, and I stared at him. I walked over and grabbed his arms and dragged him into the closet.

There was a huge six-foot mirror with an ornate frame between two of the shelf units.

"The latch has to be on the frame somewhere," said Mason.

"I already tried it," I said. I had run my fingers over the whole frame, but... did I check the sides of it? I moved my fingers to its outer edges. The button was on the very bottom, about a foot off the floor.

I pushed it, and a red outline of a right hand appeared in the bottom right corner of the mirror. I showed it to Mason.

"Palm print," he said.

I grabbed J.J. "I can choke you unconscious if I need to," I said.

He let me put his right palm, thumb and four fingers exactly where the red light asked for them.

Nothing happened.

I looked up. A red eye was now showing in the mirror, just the right height for J.J.'s eyes.

From the shape, it was clearly the image of a person's right eye.

As I lifted J.J. up, I wondered about that. Why would you go out of your way to show a visual that could only be a right eye? Why not just show an eyeball — so it wasn't clear which eye it should be?

The hand was an obvious right hand — but you couldn't disguise that. You needed the fingertips and thumb to line up with the sensors.

But an eye...

"What part of the eye do sensors read?" I asked Mason.

"The iris," he said in my ear.

"Only that?"

"Yes, why?"

I suddenly realized the fear sweat J.J. had been emitting since I brought him in here was dissipating. He was less afraid right now.

"Clever," I said, then I held him up — he couldn't stand on his own with his ankles zip-tied together — and put his *left* eye facing the red eye in the mirror.

Nothing happened.

I looked. J.J. had closed his eyes. Tightly.

I jerked him around and pushed him against a drawer unit in the closet. He was tall enough to sit on top of it, so I sat his butt on it and shoved him back. My left arm was aching from holding him up — but I couldn't let him know that.

"J.J.," I said. "Look at me."

He kept his eyes scrunched closed.

*Could I risk this?* I decided yes.

I looked at my right index finger and the bigger one next to it and willed them both to transform. They both shrank a little, then fur tufted around them. Then both fingers turned into claws.

I placed both claws on his face, right under his right eye, and started down — digging into the skin enough to draw a line of blood.

"You know you're not facing the mirror, right? I think you really need to see this."

He opened his right eye only. I pulled my claws back a little and tapped them on his nose.

His other eye shot open. I saw white all around his bulging blue eyes. His jaw dropped.

"Since I don't need your right eye to open this, I could pluck it out just for giggles."

I moved the claws to his right eye, planning to tap it instead of his nose.

He shut it tight.

"These claws will easily cut through your eyelid. I can scoop that eyeball right out."

"Okay, okay," he said. "Don't. I'll let you in."

I jerked him off the chest of drawers and back in front of the mirror, his left eye lined up with the red image on the mirror.

He must have opened his eye because I heard a soft click. The left side of the mirror moved back like a door opening. There was a room inside, big enough for a fat, comfortable-looking leather recliner. There were shelves. And a security system with a screen. And a 14x14 safe with a combination dial on the front. Plus a 2-drawer file cabinet.

I showed it all to Mason through the camera, then opened the file cabinet. There were 10 hanging file folders in the top drawer. Another 15 in the bottom. Some were fat, holding videotapes, CDs, and flash drives. Some were slim.

"Rasmussen, Alfred" was one of the files. It held notes, photos, and a flash drive labeled "A.R. Audio 1-6-13."

Suddenly, I had a big problem. I wanted these files — all of them. But I couldn't carry them away in wolf form. The only way I could get them would be to drive out of here with them.

I said to Mason, "I think we need to see what's in all these files. There could be some really horrible crimes in here that people should not get away with."

"Leave it for the feds?"

"There could be some innocents in here, too. Probably not, but maybe."

I saw movement out of the corner of my eye. J.J. was half way out of the closet, wriggling on the floor like an inch worm. I went to him, dragged him back, and lifted him into the recliner.

"Bad boy," I said to him.

"I can make you rich," J.J. said. "So rich you could never spend it all."

"Yada yada," I said. "We have millions. If we need more, we can get it."

The flummoxed look on his face made me laugh.

"Then why...?"

"You kidnapped our client. Eleven years ago, you killed her father. And, hey, you paid at least three guys to kill me."

"I get it. I'm not your favorite person. But, then, why do you want all these files?"

I could almost see the light bulbs going on inside his head. Or... rather... all the synapses firing as the big executive wheeler and dealer came to life to figure out how to solve this problem and get what he wanted. As much as he could."

"You're some kind of do-gooder, right?"

I stared at him. I was slightly interested in how he'd try to squirm out of this.

"You're one of those 'climate activists' right? You rescued your client and then you find all these records. You're thinking you could help take down a big, bad oil company. Yes?"

I said nothing.

"Well... these records are peanuts compared to what I have. What I could give you. Interested?"

"Sure."

"I've got almost double these records in another location. They could all be yours."

"In return for?"

"My freedom."

I laughed. "Not a chance."

"Okay, I can see that. In return for 24 hours. I give you the records then you let me go and wait 24 hours before you mention my name to anybody. After that...."

He shrugged. "After that you can call the cops or come after me yourselves."

He paused, watching me.

"Think about it. All the dirty politicians you can put away. And you'd have enough to take down a major oil company. Think of the congressional hearings! You'd be famous."

He looked at my face.

"Or not," he pivoted. "Depending on what you want. You could be the behind-the-scenes force that rescues the planet."

I leaned forward and patted his cheek. "J.J., we already know about your place outside of Austin, Texas. We don't need your help to get those records."

"You need my palm print. And my eye."

He looked at me and must have seen something in my face.

He gulped, and added, "I need to be alive for them to work. The screener checks."

"We don't need you for that safe," I lied. There was no way I could imagine to get him there and have him compliant. "What else you got?"

He thought and his fear stink increased.

"KDRP Oil has other facilitators. I'm not the only one. I don't know all of them, but I can give you two other names. One covers New Mexico and Oklahoma. Another covers Alaska."

I heard Mason in my ear say, "What do you think?"

Slowly, I nodded. I could see a way we could have more cake and eat it too.

I smiled.

He recoiled.

# 42

## SARA

J.J. and I negotiated.

He got to keep the cash in the room safe. It looked to be around $500,000. He also kept three passports there. I photographed two of them but allowed him to keep his identity on one of them — a Canadian passport — secret.

I got high res photos of both his eyes and both palms, even though I doubted we'd be able to use them. We emailed them from his iPad to a dropbox Mason kept.

I also took ownership of all the files from his file cabinet. I was determined to find out what other politicians KDRP owned.

We agreed I would load the files into one of the house cars, drive us both to my car, transfer the files and let him drive away in the car.

I also agreed not to report him for 24 hours.

Then I asked, "Tell me about Emily Hawking's murder."

"I didn't do it," he said. "I didn't even know about it until after it happened. She showed up out of the blue at the Houston attorney's office, and he called a local number."

I glared at him.

"I just found out yesterday. I couldn't..."

I raised my hand to shut him up.

I forced myself to continue our negotiations.

He wanted to drive his Land Rover. I wasn't letting him in that car — convinced he had built some unpleasant surprises into it. There were two Mercedes kept at the ranch for guest use, and I insisted on driving one of them.

He finally agreed if I'd move his packed go-bag from the Land Rover trunk.

I searched the go-bag. He was very prepared for the day he was caught, although I'm not sure he ever really believed it would happen. The bag, a butter-soft leather carry-on, held more money and another passport which I photographed. He had a Walther PPK (of course — it was James Bond's gun), which I emptied of ammo, and two changes of clothes. One change included a red-plaid shirt, faded jeans and a John Deere ball cap.

I lifted an eyebrow at him. "I'd pay money to see you in this disguise," I said. "You'd need a personality transplant to carry it off."

It was an hour before dawn when I sat him in the passenger seat with his legs zip-tied together and his hands tied in front and hidden under a blanket. I fastened him in with the seatbelt.

As we got close to the guard gate to exit his exclusive community, I reached down. My Spyderco knife was in a holster built into my boot. I took it out and placed it under the blanket at his groin.

Men are funny. A knife to the heart is much more of a life-and-death threat than one to the groin, but men will take much greater risks if their life is in danger than they will if it's their manhood. I didn't think women would...

Hmm... On second thought I suspected some beautiful women might choose their faces over their lives.

None of this was necessary. The guard waved us through with barely a look. They didn't seem concerned with people leaving — it was people coming in they wanted to screen.

As I drove out, J.J.'s fear stink got worse until we passed the city of Big Sky and he realized I wasn't going to drive him directly to the police.

There was no chance I would trust any local police. Not after what happened to Judy. Not with the billions of dollars this company could throw around.

"We've got a two-hour drive to my car," I told J.J. as I headed south down U.S. 191."

He recoiled. "What are you really planning to do with me? You didn't walk this distance."

"Don't worry," I said. "I hiked eight miles through the mountains. But to get there by car, we have to go almost down to West Yellowstone and then come back up 287."

He settled back, although he was still expecting a double-cross.

Was I planning one? I wasn't sure what I would do when we reached my car.

I'd have to find out when we got there. In the meantime, I wanted to learn more about what Judy had dug up about KDRP.

"So," I said, "we've got two hours. I read your CEO is new best buddies with the president of Buchestan, which is sitting on the biggest oil reserves in the Caspian Sea area. Tell me everything you know about their dealings."

I switched on my phone recording app and drove the mostly deserted road lit first by my headlights and then by the rising sun. I listened to stories of summer palaces, dachas, unimaginable wealth and total paranoia.

Uneasy rests the head of a man who achieved power through assassination.

Two hours later, J.J. and I split smoothly, despite both of us expecting the worst.

I got the files into my car. He gave me the names of two other KDPR Vice Presidents who were working the politicians in North Dakota/Alaska and in Oklahoma/New Mexico. I snipped off the zip ties and handed him his car keys.

We each stood by our respective cars and stared at each other.

He said, "You're really going to do this?"

"I'm betting there's nowhere you can hide that I can't find you."

He tilted his head. "I guess we'll see."

I waited for him to get into his car first, but he just stood there.

He said, "One last question?"

"What?"

"How'd you do that claw thing?" He held out his index and middle finger, curved like claws.

I grinned. "I've got a Hollywood special effects guy who makes Halloween costumes on the side. He's amazing, isn't he?"

"Amazing," he agreed, nodding slowly.

I looked at my watch. "Twenty-four hours starting right now."

He nodded, got in the SUV and drove away.

"He's gone," I said into my mike. "Do you think I did the right thing?"

"We can find him. He won't escape."

"I'm counting on you for that."

I sighed. "J.J. got my license plate — no way to prevent that."

"I figured," said Mason. "Judy's got a helicopter out of Bozeman on standby. Want it?"

"Have it pick me up in Ennis. I'll be there in about 25 minutes. Have her get me a charter to Tulsa from Bozeman."

"She's got them on standby, too."

"Of course she does. She runs circles around both of us."

"You, probably. Not me."

I grinned. "Okay, not you."

# 43

SARA

I t was three in the afternoon by the time I got back home. I was exhausted, dragging so badly I almost crashed my van on the way from the airport. I threw my stuff on the floor and sat in my leather recliner for just a second.

I woke up at six the next morning.

My house feels like a mausoleum without my wolf-dog Skidi there. When I'm away, she boards at Tulsa's Adventure Doggie Day Care & Kennels.

I was there first thing when it opened at eight A.M.

The place has dog pools and agility equipment, so I know Skidi has fun when I'm away. I'm convinced I miss her more than she misses me.

But this time felt like months away instead of just... was it really only 11 days?

I sat in the van with her and hugged and petted her while getting wet, slobbery dog kisses all over me. I needed every one of them.

Skidi went with me to the office, where the whole team was waiting and where she got even more pets and attention.

Connor was there, sitting carefully with a leg up on the coffee table. He stared at Skidi with a curious look. It was the same look on his face as when he was helicoptered away from Mason and the wolf that had protected him.

This might become a problem.

I shook my head to clear it.

Judy came straight from the airport and told me she'd already arranged for her cat, Lola, to come home.

Mason told us his mother was home resting and doing well.

"What's happening with the water-rights vote today?" Judy asked.

"I just spoke to Rasmussen," I said. "He knows his blackmailer has mysteriously left the country, and he can vote against it like he and most of Montana's ranchers want to."

I thought for a moment. "Judy, can you just track it and let me know in case there are any surprises?"

"Sure. But is he going to get away with what he did? You got him to talk by telling him we wouldn't come after him — but it's not right."

I nodded. "He got Otto killed and Dakota kidnapped. I'm going to tell Bill Hanalho about his part in all of this. The Lupiti Nation can decide what's right for him."

I leaned back in my chair and looked at each of the team. "This case has a lot of loose ends," I said. "Let's figure out what, if anything, we want to do about the rest of them."

Judy said, "Finding Dakota's mother has to be first. I'm worried Dakota might even go back to Montana looking for her. She's not answering her phone today."

"She's likely had bad news," I said, pulling out my phone and showing them a small item in yesterday's *Tulsa World* about a murdered man and a dead woman pulled from a Houston bayou.

"I'm pretty sure this woman is her mother. The Houston police probably contacted her yesterday."

Three heads turned to look at me accusingly.

"Don't look at me," I said. "I didn't do it."

"Girl," Judy said, "None of us would think you'd killed *her*."

I ignored her and said, "Mason and I were keeping an eye on Houston because he found a phone call Emily made to the questionable 'insurance' guy there who was sending her checks. When she disappeared, we thought she might have gone there."

Connor popped his knuckles and said, "The biggest loose end I see is what we do about all the politicians being blackmailed by KDRP Oil. I looked through some of those files, and it's hard to stomach the scope of their blackmail. What we have shows the votes they bought in Montana and Texas, but it's obvious they're doing it in most of the other states as well. We can't ignore it."

"No, we can't," I agreed. "But we're not the right group to do anything about it. We help people in physical peril. Handling these files requires a whole different skill set."

"I've been thinking about that," Judy said. "Newspapers used to have teams of investigative reporters — but today it's only a few. And those few specialize in subjects, like medicine."

"Big oil has billions to spend," Connor said. "They could destroy a newspaper. Who would risk it?"

"Our best bet," said Judy, "is Greenpeace. Their entire mission is centered on the environment. Their UK-based Unearthed is the group that secretly recorded ExxonMobile executives talking about their support for "shadow groups" that plant doubt about the damage big oil is doing to the environment."

I looked and saw nods all around the table.

"Make a backup copy for us," I told her, "then give what we have to them. Including the names of the company VPs running the blackmail schemes in New Mexico/Oklahoma and North Dakota/Alaska. But tell them it's on one condition — they have to publish from at least one of these files within 30 days. Something they could only have gotten from a blackmail tape."

"Why?"

"J.J. Andersen is our biggest loose end. He ordered Judy and Dakota taken, and he ordered Otto Hawking's death. He does not get away with this."

I saw nods all around the table.

"But," I added, "we can't go after every murdering bad guy — there are too many of them. I want to save us for when someone is in danger — someone we can rescue.

"When Greenpeace publishes, the president of KDRP — Augustus Kingsley — will learn that J.J. has given the press one of his secret files. Kingsley will have to wonder how many other files J.J. might deliver. Meanwhile, Mason will find out where he's hiding and make sure KDRP learns of it.

"If KDRP is as ruthless as it appears, they will take out J.J."

I looked around and saw some smiles. Also a lot of relief.

"This case kicked our butts," I said. "We got stabbed," I nodded at Connor, "kidnapped," I looked at Judy, "and pummeled," I nodded at Mason and pointed at my chest, "more than we've faced before."

"We won. But we paid for it. Let's all take some serious time off. I can't promise another urgent case won't drop in our laps soon — but let's pretend it won't. Go somewhere. Do something that matters to you. Get laid. Get married. Do whatever makes you happy."

"Well... if you *insist*," Judy said, laughing.

Connor had grinned, but then shook his head. "You're leaving one loose end — Augustus Kingsley. You can't believe the CEO of KDRP was innocent in all of this?"

I shook my head. "No, I don't believe he's innocent. But neither do I have proof."

"C'mon!"

I raised my hand. "Think about it. All of you." I made eye contact with each of them. "While we focus on rescuing people, in many ways we're a vigilante group."

I paused to let that sink in.

"The worst thing," I continued, "about vigilantes is they become so self-righteous that one day they take down an innocent person. I refuse to ever risk that — I need to be able to sleep at night.

"So... Augustus Kingsley gets this test. He discovers the murders and blackmail J.J. was ordering — if he didn't already know it — and then he discovers where the man is hiding. Then what happens? Does J.J. keep enjoying his retirement? Or is he murdered?

Judy smiled. "And if he's murdered..."

"Exactly."

Connor frowned. "If Kingsley has him murdered, then what happens to Kingsley?"

I shrugged. "Like I said, we can't go around killing all the bad guys in the world. But if they want to kill each other off — it's just dandy with me."

"Meaning?" Connor wasn't letting this go.

"KDRP does a lot of business around the Caspian Sea — with Russia and Kazakhstan. But lately, Kingsley has become the BFF of Igor Gutulyev, the president-for-life of Buchestan — which has the largest proven oil reserves in the region.

"Two years ago, Buchestan's prime minister decided he would be a better choice to be president and he managed to get some of the army behind him. Three days later the prime minister and his supporters — and his family — were all dead."

Connor raised his eyebrows. "Oh."

Judy shook her head. "I don't get it, y'all."

Connor looked at Mason, who thus far had said only two words in this meeting. I wasn't sure he was paying attention.

Connor said to him, "Does Kingsley go to Buchestan often?"

Mason nodded. "He's been over there twice in the last six months."

Connor finally smiled a big grin, one that would make most people run and hide. "Dictators stay in power by being paranoid. The right word in the right ear..."

Mason stood up. "I'm hanging around here for a couple of days for Emily Hawking's funeral. And to find where J.J. is hiding. Then, I'm taking Sara up on her suggestion. I'm heading to Alaska — for personal business. I don't know how long I'll be gone, but you all have my number."

We all stood up as well.

Judy said, "I've got a beau with one of those huge RVs. I'm fixing' to let him take Lola and me to Tennessee. I always wanted to see Dollywood. She's been a hero of mine forever. But y'all have my number. I'll be back quick if you need me."

I raised my eyebrows at Connor. He shrugged. "I'll talk to Lillian. Maybe we'll go somewhere."

Judy asked, "What about you, Sara?"

I twisted my mouth. "It's past time I had a heart-to-heart with somebody."

She raised an eyebrow at me. She knew about Bill Hanalho.

I nodded at her and she smiled.

Connor shook hands with Mason. When he extended one to me, I pulled him in for a hug. Judy one-upped me by pulling him into her arms and planting a big kiss on his cheek.

Then I went home and crashed into bed with Skidi. Amazingly, I was still tired. It was just six P.M. when we hit the sack, but I slept through the night. It felt warm and familiar and comforting, although....

I woke up once — convinced I was back sleeping with my wolf pack in Yellowstone.

# 44

## SARA

Two days later, the four of us attended Emily Hawking's funeral.

I didn't know anything about Lupiti death practices, but I learned there was fasting (Dakota, not us), prayers, songs and smudging. They didn't believe in embalming, so Emily was kept chilled through dry ice. She was buried in a simple cedar coffin.

Bill Hanalho was there, presiding over the service and helping Dakota.

The ritual made me ashamed of how I'd buried Joe White Wolf, the neighbor who had turned me three years ago.

Joe had cut his chest with a ceremonial knife, and when I moved to stem the bleeding, he'd cut my hand and held it to his bloody chest. Then he said he was sorry, and he turned his head to a wall. He wouldn't eat, speak, or respond to me in any way. He died within the hour — as if he'd willed it.

Tending to him in his house, I'd had my first view of a room whose door had always been closed to me. Inside he had relics and two very old books that were written in Lupiti. The bindings of those books looked like skin.

I freaked with his death and the "sharing of blood" thing. Instead of calling anybody, I carried his body up higher into the Colorado foothills and buried him with no casket. I didn't know what to say over him, but I did light a tiny fire and blow smoke over where he lay.

Watching the care given to laying Emily to rest, I realized Joe deserved better. He had been the tribe's shaman for decades until he left them.

I resolved to tell Bill what I'd done and ask what he'd recommend we do.

Two days later, Bill called and asked to meet at the entrance to the Fair Grounds. When he drove up, I was standing, leaning against the Fair Grounds sign, watching students run track at the high school next door.

No wonder nobody else appeals to me, I thought, as I watched him walk towards me. The guy's a frigging wet dream. The midnight black hair swaying in the wind. The large, sinewy body — not muscle-pumped, but very strong. The intelligence in his eyes. The heart of him — the way he cares for people. How he tries to help them.

"Hey, Bill," I said.

"Hey, Sara. Let's walk." He turned away from the school, and we strolled past an empty row of horse stalls, over towards the ring where the annual rodeo is held.

"Let me tell you something first," I said as we walked. "The man who actually killed Otto Hawking is dead. The man he worked for, J.J. Andersen, the man who ordered Dakota taken — he'll soon be out of the picture.

"That leaves a man named Al Rasmussen. He's a big landowner in Montana, and he's on the Montana Energy Review Board. He killed his father for money — to stop him from putting a conservation easement on the 200-plus acres of land he owned — land which Al then inherited.

"Otto overheard their fight so Rasmussen asked J.J. to 'fix' it, and he did."

Bill furrowed his eyebrows at me.

"I'm telling this to you as a representative of the Lupiti Nation. I and my team aren't doing anything about Rasmussen. But none of this — Otto's death and Dakota's kidnapping — would have happened without him."

Bill was quiet, so I looked over at him.

"Understood."

We reached the fencing around the rodeo grounds, and Bill leaned his back against it.

I put my hands on the top rung and a boot up on the lower. I could almost see the women on horseback who competed in this ring, chasing after a calf, lassoing it, leaping from their horses to hogtie its legs and competing to score the fastest time.

"Sara," he said.

I turned.

He took a breath. "I'm getting married next month. She's a good Lupiti woman and we intend to raise a family."

He took another breath and turned away from me. "You know it's my duty to the tribe."

I stood there. Speechless. Staring at the back of his head.

It felt like I was in an earthquake. The ground under me turned unstable. Gravity disappeared and my stomach shot into my throat.

I wanted to throw up.

Very quietly I said, "You couldn't wait a year?"

He turned back to me, anguish on his face. "If we took that year, it would be worse. It might hurt so bad I could never do this. And I *have* to do this."

He clutched my shoulders, willing me to understand. "The tribe needs a priest now. And even more so in the future."

Seeing him so close... feeling his hands on my shoulders...

I knew it was wrong, but...

I leaned forward into him. I grabbed his face with my hands.

I kissed him. Not hard, but not a peck. I kissed him with love and tenderness. And with tears.

He stood there, letting me. *My god, how could one man's lips be so soft?*

Doing nothing.

Then his arms snapped around me like a steel trap, mashing me to him. He kissed me back — hard.

He kissed like a man who was starved for oxygen, and I had the only supply of it.

His hands went everywhere. He used them to cup the back of my head, mashing it against him. He grabbed my waist. My ass. He ground me against him.

I had the same problem. I ran my fingers through his hair like I'd craved for years. I hugged him to me as tight as I could.

Our tongues met.

The heat was killing me. Fire burned all around us, the flames licking my body.

It seared my skin.

I couldn't breathe.

I was having a heart attack.

And I was wrong to do this. Dead wrong.

Crying sharply in pain, I pushed back from him. I gasped for air.

And then I did something truly evil.

I couldn't stop myself because I knew none of what we'd done would change the fact of his marriage.

"Enjoy your wife," I said, then I turned and walked away.

I did not look back, but it took every bit of willpower I still possessed. I kept walking right to my van.

I drove home, packed up my house, grabbed Skidi and got back in the van.

I headed north to Alaska. Not to wherever Mason was going — I felt completely antisocial. In fact, I wanted to find a human-free zone.

Maybe I'd go stay on some of the land I'd been buying up with my share of the money we were making. I wanted to end up with at least 400 acres in Alaska — which I would turn into an animal sanctuary for the wolves.

Maybe I'd live in wolf form for awhile. Maybe that would hurt less.

Maybe, as a wolf, I wouldn't feel the overpowering guilt that was hounding me.

I knew what I'd done was wrong. The pain I'd felt was crushing and I'd lashed out — I wanted him to hurt as I did.

But I also — desperately — had to know what I was going to miss.

Was what I felt for him really as powerful as it had seemed all this time?

I laughed, bitterly.

Wasn't there a Chinese curse or something that said — watch out what you wish for because you might get it?

Well I got it alright. I knew the answer now.

And I'd have to live the rest of my life with that pain.

# 45

## BOZEMAN DAILY CHRONICLE

February 9 — Montana landowner Alfred Rasmussen is missing. He was last seen two days ago, leaving home for a meeting at the Montana Energy Review Board, but he never arrived. If you have information about this case, please contact your local law enforcement agency.

# 46

## TULSA WORLD — NATIONAL NEWS

August 14 — KDRP Oil & Gas CEO Augustus Kingsley was killed today in Buchestan. A car carrying Kingsley and two other KDRP executives crashed into a truck on a bridge just outside the capital city of Elkaclia, smashed through the barrier, and fell into the river below. There were no survivors.

THE END

# FREE STORY DOWNLOAD
## NOT AVAILABLE IN ANY STORE!

**Werewolves and Holidays**

Sometimes I write poor Sara Flores into a corner and even I can't figure out how she's going to survive. That's when I take a week off and write a short story. Typically about her and some holiday.

I offer the story exclusively to anyone who joins my monthly author mailing list.

As I write this in January, 2024, the story is *Suzy's Very Bad Valentine's Day*.

Because you may be reading this at an entirely different time of the year, let me recommend you go to: SueDenver.com.

**Right on the home page there will be a story for a current holiday and a signup to get it for free.**

Also… with 19,000 books being launched in just the U.S. each week, joining this list will make sure you don't miss the next Sara Flores book when it comes out.

# SUE DENVER BOOKS AVAILABLE EVERYWHERE

## SERIES: Sara Flores, Werewolf P.I.

**BOOK ONE:** *New Private Investigator Sara Flores is up to her werewolf snout in hired assassins and explosives while trying to save her first client's life.* [146-page novella]

**BOOK TWO:** Sara was hired to find a woman who left her Tulsa casino job 192 days ago - and hasn't been seen since. The cops say Alaska Brown left willingly. The FBI isn't looking. And now, someone deadly is trying to kill off Sara and her team. Someone with unlimited funds. Can Sara and her 3-person team of misfits really take down a billionaire — or is this the case that gets them all killed? [260 pgs.]

**BOOK THREE:** Sara Flores, werewolf P.I., needs to find a young woman who disappeared seeking evidence her father was murdered 12 years ago — instead of dying drugged and stupid in a Wyoming snowstorm. But to do that, Sara has to confront a man who even U.S. presidents have been afraid to touch.

# SERIES: Sara Flores, the Early Years

*BOOK ONE: Sara's first 8 adventures (short stories & one novella) from her origin story through the end of her first year as a werewolf. See her transform herself into an avenger of the powerless and into evildoers worst nightmare.* [204 pages]

*BOOK TWO: Year 2 for Sara includes three novellas:* **BETRAYAL IN OKLAHOMA** *(Sara's going to save that little boy if she has to bite the heads off half the criminals in the state. Literally.),* **THE STENCH OF FEAR** *(Sara's after a man who's working with the cops. She can't stop because they're killing women), and* **AMATEUR ASSASSIN** *(Sara faces the ethical dilemma of her life. Should a man die for what he will do?)* [210 pages]

# AFTERWORD

A big part of the fun of being an author is the research you get to do. In trying to find ways for Judy to defend herself without having to punch anybody, I went down a rabbit hole into hat pins.

They became popular with women in the very early 1900s as women first moved into the workplace and found themselves harassed by men at work or traveling to and from work.

However... some men found this self-defense very objectionable and wrote editorials about the dangers of hat-pin-wielding women. See the attached from a newspaper of the time.

# The Hat Pin Peril

Growing Danger in City Crowds That Places a Startling List of Accidents Beside the Long Record of Violent Assaults Committed With Woman's Deadly Weapon.

of the woman sitting behind him, declares that she had stabbed him in the shoulder. Th...

# ABOUT THE AUTHOR

Did you ever want to be more than yourself? I always have. As a kid, I imagined I lived up in the clouds with a band of other kids. We would swoop down — because we could fly! — and rescue people in trouble. And we'd beat the crap out of their abusers.

When I got older, I became obsessed with crime and mysteries. I wanted to know how someone could track down evil doers and peel back their false faces — exposing them to the world.

The day I quit my corporate job — my dreams came true. Today I spend my time throwing my character, Sara Flores, at one criminal mastermind after another — just to see what she can do.

And... I cheated. I let her be more than herself by making her a werewolf — the only magical creature in a world otherwise just like ours. Because I wanted to see what she could do with a wolf's senses and strength. And wildness.

So join me for stories of ruthless criminals, suspicious cops, and Sara's small band of misfits fighting to save us all at SueDenver.com.

WolfLady.net

instagram.com/wolfladydotnet

tiktok.com/@wolfladysuedenver

youtube.com/@suedenverauthor

amazon.com/Sue-Denver/e/B096KVQ12D?ref=sr_ntt_s-rch_lnk_1&qid=1642709028&sr=8-1

bookbub.com/authors/sue-denver

goodreads.com/suedenvercom

www.ingramcontent.com/pod-product-compliance
Lightning Source LLC
Chambersburg PA
CBHW052034020726
47501CB00004B/1398